Receive a free short story set in the HARD PLACE world when
you sign up for
the HARD PLACE newsletter.
Go to Deadcatstud.io

A COLD HAND

A COLLECTION OF STORIES
FROM A HARD PLACE
VOLUME 3
BY R A JACOBSON

THECROSSROADDEAL.COM

"Any deal is better than no deal. Isn't it?"

Contents

Note

Dear reader,
Two of the stories are reprints from past collections. THE RIDE from A
SINGLE ROUND and PASSING IT FORWARD from A LEAD PILL are reprinted
here to give context to the stories, OUT OF ROAD and A QUESTION OF PAYMENT.

Enjoy
R A J
Nov 2022

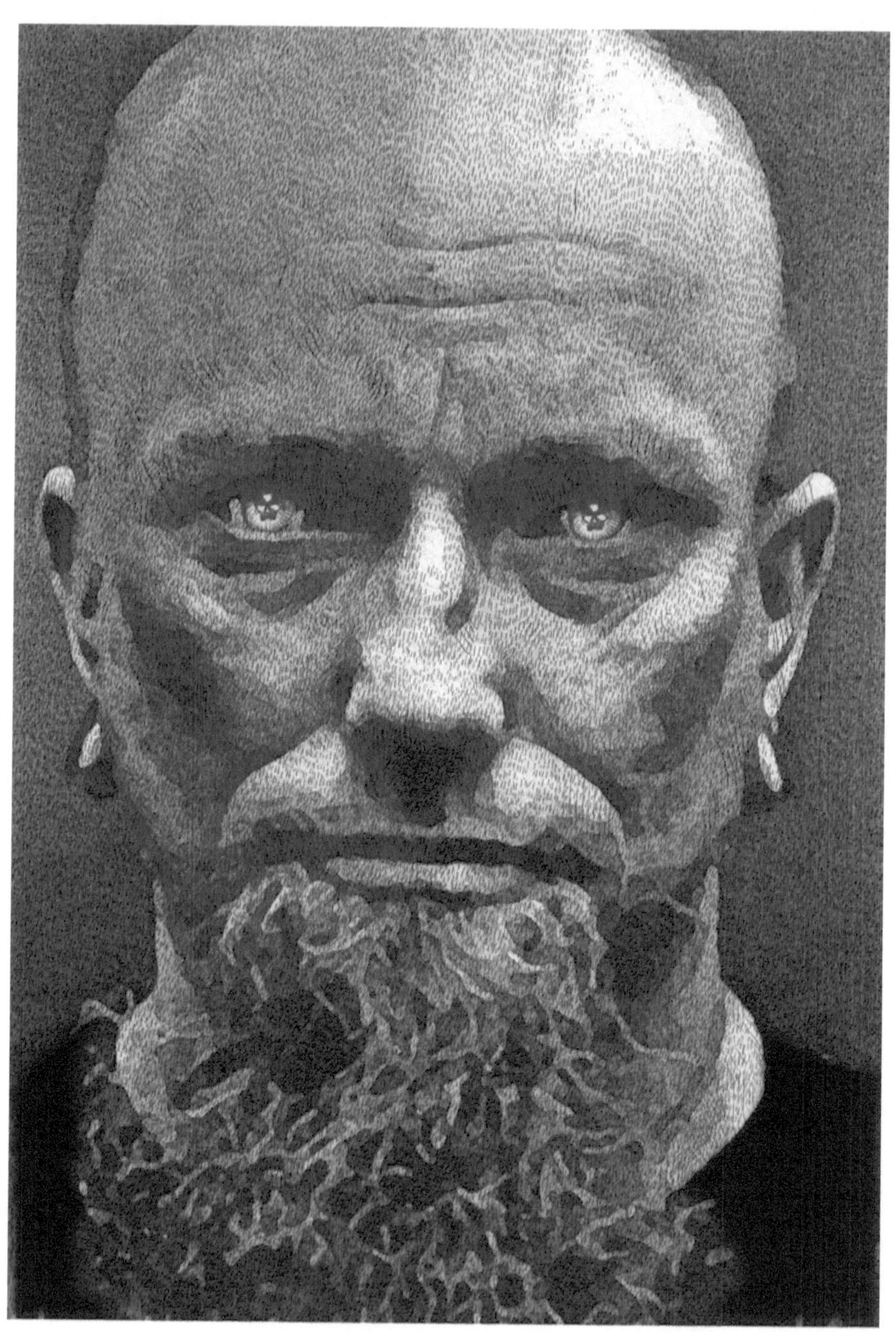

Frank stared at him for a long time, then he broke.

1

FRANK

1 SCRATCH IN TIME

The SCRATCH IN TIME was a small, cozy coffee shop on a backstreet. Its dark wood-panelled walls, creamy plastered ceiling, lazy ceiling fan and multi-paned window echoed a distant past. Frank, the owner, was an easy-going man with a quick smile, a slight hippy vibe, and an enormous belly. He lived in a small apartment above the cafe that he spent almost no time in instead spending mostly in the cafe. He had named it after his cat, Scratch. The cat had been a fixture in the cafe, sliding up to every new person who visited. Curling around their legs, sitting on the arms of the big armchairs in the window soaking up the sun and the attention of the coffee drinkers. The regulars loved Scratch and would come in just to say hello, but six years ago, Scratch passed away. Frank had been heartbroken. He loved Scratch. He put a photo above the counter, then another by the sugar, cream and stir sticks, still another by the till. One slow afternoon, he hung over a dozen beautiful shots of Scratch on the exposed brick wall. They looked great, and he felt it honoured Scratch.

The regulars missed Scratch as well and loved the photos. One day, a regular, a man named Joseph, brought in a framed photo of his cat that had passed away two days ago and asked if he could hang it next to Scratch's photo. Frank was reluctant, feeling it would take away from Scratch's memory, but he said he would think about it, took the photo, and Joseph left. That night, after he had closed the cafe down for the night, Frank looked at the wall covered with photos of his beloved Scratch. He sat in the dark for a long while, staring, and he cried. He realised he could not remember Scratch except by the photos. He had nothing else. He couldn't remember her purring or meowing. He couldn't remember anything other than the still frozen moments hung on the wall.

He looked at the photo of Joseph's cat. It looked like any other cat. Nothing special, just a cat, like Scratch. He put Joseph's cat's photo up beside Scratch.

A couple of days later, Joseph came in and was overjoyed to see his cat honoured up next to Scratch.

A few days later, a woman came in with a photo of her cat. Frank smiled and hung it on the wall next to Scratch. After a few weeks, the wall was full. His regulars, the ones who had known Scratch, brought in photos of their cats. Frank started hanging them on other walls. Eventually, the walls were covered with pet photos. Cats mostly, but there were dogs, birds and even a spotted green lizard.

On a rainy Saturday, Frank was sitting behind the counter rereading his favourite book, glancing up every so often. Despite being a perfect day to relax in a cafe by the window, read, drink coffee, and watch the world go by outside, the room was nearly empty. All the comfy armchairs by the windows were occupied with individuals doing just that.

Several times people came in, looked longingly at the armchairs, and ordered their coffee to go. A few more persistent individuals sat for a while at a table, waiting for a treasured spot to open. Some were rewarded. Others finished their coffee and left disappointed.

A man stepped in, shaking his umbrella. He leaned it against the wall and looked around. Seeing Frank, he smiled and stepped up to the counter. Halfway there he noticed the cat photos that filled the walls. He stood staring for a time, smiled a small smile, looked at the sandwiches, pastries on display, and after a second, he looked up at Frank.

"Hi," he looked back down at the glass case and paused, "Umm, I guess just a coffee." He looked up past Frank to the Chalkboard. After several minutes, he glanced at the cat photos, frowned.

"Sure. Do you want 'dark roast' or maybe an Americano?" Frank coxed.

The man looked down, "Umm, just a dark roast, thanks," he smiled, "with cream."

"The cream and sugar are over there." Frank pointed to a small counter with lids, napkins, stir sticks, and cream.

"Oh yes, of course," he looked at the counter, then looked back at Frank, "Hey, did you know there's a burger joint called 'From Scratch' over on 17th?" He said, but Frank couldn't hear. He could see the man's lips moving. Tiny points of light were popping in his eyes, and a migraine was starting. Through the pain, Frank smiled as the man went on. Something about a burger place. Frank tried to concentrate, but it was no use.

Frank smiled and mumbled. "No, I didn't know. That's cool." and handed the man his coffee.

The man looked at Frank, then frowning, went to the counter with the cream and dressed his coffee. He glanced at Frank as he opened the door and left. A second later, the door opened again. The man reached back in and grabbed his umbrella, glanced at the cat wall, then at Frank as the door closed.

Frank's headache vanished as quickly as it had started.

On a Tuesday afternoon, two men stepped into the cafe. They were tall, thin, and dressed in black suits. They immediately made Frank think of a pair of giant spiders, although he thought their broad-brimmed hats were a bit much. The door closed behind them. They stood shoulder to shoulder, scanning the room with slow, deliberate movements. After a second, in unison, their heads focused on Frank. They walked in step up to him. As he watched them approach, the back of his neck prickled.

"Frank?" They asked in unison. Their voices, high and flute-like, seemed out of place.

"Yes?" Frank responded, unsure. His headache thundered back, wrapping his brain in a fierce grip. Blackness swam around his vision, creeping in from the edges of sight. He watched those black hats move as the two men spoke. He knew they were speaking, but he couldn't seem to understand. He picked out a word or two, but what it meant, he couldn't have said. He watched slack jawed as they turned and walked out as they had come, moving as mirror images. Frank felt like he may throw up. His stomach did backflips. Steadying himself on the counter, he stared at the door. A weird unease, a feeling of an impending deadline, clawed at his brain, but he could not think of anything he had forgotten. Through a sick haze, he sifted through his memory.

Frank looked around at the cafe, at the people enjoying a Tuesday afternoon in his comfortable cafe. It all looked so peaceful, so safe, but... but it was a lie. It was all a lie.

Frank staggered slightly, then leaned on the counter as he stared at the wall of cat photos. It was all a lie! It was early afternoon, and the cafe would usually be busy, but the room slowly emptied, and by four, he was alone in his cafe. It had never happened, not since he opened. He stood behind the counter, feeling panicked and still sick. After a half-hour, he decided he wasn't feeling well enough. He put the closed sign on the door and went upstairs to lie down.

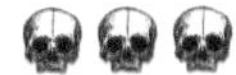

2 SCRATCHING OUT A LIVING

Frank hated Tuesday nights. Tuesday was karaoke night at the Scratching Post. It brought in a lot of customers, but the chose the same songs over and over by mostly horrendous singers. Dead cat squalling, ruining songs he loved and now could no longer listen to.

The nights were dreadful enough that he had purchased earplugs that cut out the noise. They helped, but not enough. His ear rang the rest of the night while he tried to sleep and much of the next day.

That wasn't the worst of it. The worst part was the loss of his favourite songs, songs that before that hated machine had been special to him. Many of the songs in the Karaoke machine were awful, but a few were songs he really enjoyed.

'… had enjoyed,' he thought bitterly.

When he first purchased the machine, he went into the settings to remove songs he didn't want to hear.

After a couple of nights, he realised he should have removed the songs he loved to protect them, to save them from the onslaught.

Now, of course, it was too late. They were ruined. Every Tuesday pushed them further from him, making the songs poison in his ears. At one time, after everyone had left for the night and the bar was closed, empty and quiet, he would play his music loud and move about, not dancing but moving with the beat. Now he still loved his bar most when it was closed, but now he enjoyed it silently.

Tuesday night continued. It brought a full house every time. He got so he could guess what music he would have to endure when someone walked through the front door of his bar. He could tell if they would choose Celine Dion or Michael Bublé or even Brian Adams. Or he was about to be serenaded by a version of Tears of Heaven or Barbie world or, even worse, Margaritaville. It became his game, the only thing he could find to get him through till 1:30 when he closed and could go home, his ears and brain ringing. He would stay in a shitty mood until Friday night, when he had live music that washed the taste of Tuesday away.

The best Fridays were when he booked a band that called themselves Rio Grande Mud. They were a very good ZZ Top cover band. When they played, he grinned for most of the weekend. It almost made the next Tuesday bearable.

He was standing behind the bar, early on a dreaded Tuesday, watching the room as it slowly filled, grimly bracing himself for his weekly onslaught.

Two men stepped through the door and paused. Frank noticed them immediately. They stood out, dressed alike in dark suits and big hats. They grinned at the room with gigantic smiles, filled with white teeth that made Frank think of the grill of some antique car just before it ran him over. He shuddered at the thought and tried to guess what song would be theirs. He couldn't come up with a song for them. They really didn't look like karaoke torturers, just maybe torturers of a different kind.

Their heads swung across the room and locked on Frank. Their grins broadened as they walked toward him with matched strides. Frank suddenly felt nervous. He straightened. Smiling, they walked to him and started talking. Frank heard his name, then nothing more.

Over the last few months, the ringing in his ears had gotten worse, making sleep more challenging each night. It was called tinnitus. From what he had read, it progressed slowly over time as the damage compounded, but now the ringing exploded in his head. A tooth rattling screech that drowned out everything else. Frank squinted and tipped his ear toward the smiling men. He could not hear a word. He put his finger in his ear and wiggled it roughly, trying to clear the noise away as he watched their wide, smiling mouths move. They talked for several minutes. With a nod and a smile, they turned and left the bar. As he watched the door close, the ringing fell away. His eyes closed tightly as he leaned into his hands. He opened them just as six laughing women walked in. He groaned, happy to have the customers. Unhappy about the night of torture he was going to endure, all the while smiling, acting like he was enjoying the catawolling.

It was worse than he had expected. About an hour later, another group of happy, half-drunk women flooded in. Within minutes, the same songs were repeated. Why do they always choose the same songs? He could count on hearing at least once in an evening, often more Billie Jean, Don't Stop Believin', Dancing Queen, and I Wanna Dance with Somebody. It was painfully inevitable.

Frank kept a bottle of Advil under the counter. By the end of the evening, he was popping them like candy. He sat down, relieved when the last group staggered out, and he locked it behind them.

These nights were getting harder to tolerate. His head each Tuesday had become so painful he wasn't sure he would survive the next. He was determined to look over the numbers and see if it really was worth it.

An hour later, he shut the lights off and walked outside, enjoying the cool night air. Standing looking at the empty street, listening to the quiet, frustrated by the constant ringing in his ears that he knew would keep him awake. After Hell night, he didn't sleep well. He walked around back and climbed the stairs to his apartment above his bar, knowing that he could never escape Tuesdays. He couldn't afford to.

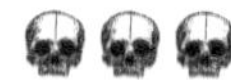

3 OL' TOM'S BACKROOM

Frank had run the Backroom for over six years. His burgers had been written up in many local newspapers and had gotten rave reviews on food podcasts and blogs, but what made his joint famous wasn't his food. It had been famous for many years long before he got it. No, it was famous for its backroom called Ol' Tom's Backroom. It had been started by the previous owners years ago and it had become the place to go for live music soon after it was opened. Every Wednesday night, the Backroom hosted an open mic for the up-and-coming musicians. Live acts that were, if not famous, certainly on their way to being famous. Over the years, several legends surrounded the open stage. One was that Bob Dylan had played one song when Ol' Tom's Backroom had just opened. Another claimed that a musician named John 'Whitey' Burnet played for the Devil and vanished that very night.

Frank loved having a restaurant that had even a small amount of fame. He was sure it was all BS, but he did everything he could to play it up. He started changing the names of his food to Devil themed names, giving rise to the Diablo burger, the Perdition burger, and Blackened Hell flamed wings.

Frank could be found every night in the open kitchen, his back to the restaurant part of the bar, the flames of his grill heating his face. Occasionally, he'd look up to see when someone came in. He would give them a big friendly smile, wave with his spatula and return to the flattop.

On Wednesdays, after the supper crowd had slowed around 8, the people that walked through the door inevitably carried a guitar case, so it surprised him to see two men walk in smiling hugely with dark large brimmed hats and no guitar cases.

They walked straight up to the bar, ignoring the tiny server who asked them if they would like a seat, and asked for Frank.

Frank turned, already annoyed by whatever this was.

"My name is Mr. July, and this is Mr. January. You are Frank, the owner of this fine establishment," Mr. July said with a broad smile.

"Ya, what do you want?" Frank said, wiping his hands on a cloth.

"We are here concerning…." the man began but just then, from the Backroom, the PA system let out a horrible feedback screech, then someone with very little guitar skills ran up the neck trying to be Stevie or something. Frank watched the smiling mouth flap away under that ridiculous hat, but he couldn't hear a word of it. When the brutalization of the guitar ended, and Frank could hear again, the man was finishing.

"We will return in two weeks to fulfill your contract's clause. Have a wonderful evening," he said, and with broad smiles, they turned in unison and left. Frank watched them go, looked at the server, who shrugged. He shook his head and went back to the grill. "Never know what kind Fuckin weird shit will walk through the door," he said to the meat he wasn't cooking to perfection. He glanced back to where the two had left. He shook his head once more, then checked out the young server's ass. He may have to make a grab for that before the night was over.

4 SCRATCHING POST

Frank stepped into the elevator just after four-thirty in a perfectly tailored suit of gunmetal grey and a crisp white shirt open at the neck. He checked his watch. He had still an hour before opening, and he knew the day shift would be in the kitchen prepping.

He leaned back against the mirrored wall and closed his eyes. Wednesday nights could go anyway. When he had first thought of having an open mic night, he had envisioned famous jazz musicians casually dropping by to try out their newest scrambled egg variations and some nights; the stars aligned. The energy was perfect, and the music was wonderful. Every act that stepped on stage was new and original, not always jazz but still enjoyable. Other nights were the exact opposite. One act after another assaulted his ears. Badly done with covers that should have been left alone. He had come to dread the open stage more than he had once looked forward to it. If only there were enough jazz quartets to fill his evenings that he could do away with the open stage.

When he opened his eyes, he was looking at himself. He examined the figure that was his constant companion. His reflection was the same, never changing, but somehow, he looked like a stranger that sort of looked like himself. He looked tight. His outfit was entirely in shades of grey, suit, shirt, and tie, all as uniform as he could manage. He brushed at a small fuzz on his lapel. Tight, yes, he looked tight, but he knew just below the surface of control was a rage, an uncontrollable fire that frightened him. It was as if there was a second being that he shared this body with.

The elevator slid open. With a sigh, Frank pushed himself from the wall and walked across the lobby to the rain-slick street. It had rained most of the night and the heavy, dark clouds threatened to open up.

He opened his restaurant almost six years ago and, for the first few years, had lived above it in the small apartment there. Now as he walked the half block to his restaurant, it had stopped. The air weighed on him, and he could feel the edges of a headache.

The restaurant felt right when he entered. He could hear the kitchen staff prepping. It made him smile. Out front, he had two servers. One was new. She seemed to pick things up quickly. He enjoyed watching the staff moving through their tasks efficiently and with economy. Nothing wasted, nothing overdone. He could feel the dichotomy in him, the feeling of being slit, as if his soul was divided in half. One here and present and one somewhere else, seeing another world, another time. He strolled from room to room, his ever-present notebook in hand and checking off his list as always, but this night had an edge like a vintage tapestry, its edges frayed and dwindling. Inside, he smiled as he entered one of the two formal dining rooms and the clatter of the servers setting tables hushed instantly. His cool presence had the effect he wanted. These rooms were only sporadically booked; however, he could not let them go. The idea of an upscale dining room was, for him, an extension of his vision, his dream. There was nothing to be done. He would have to give up on this dream. The books told him. There was no way to keep them open. The money just wasn't there. What the Scratching Post needed was not fancy dining rooms, but more room for people to drink, cheap fast food, and entertainment to bring them in.

He passed the large mirror behind the bar, and once again caught his own eyes. He appraised what he saw there. He was a fool. His aspirations and affectations were going to lose him the Bar he had worked so hard to buy.

His brow furrowed. He looked to the ground and tried to recall. He had worked hard to buy this bar, hadn't he? He had opened the bar just over six years ago. He could remember that. He was sure of that, just over six years ago. Every time he stopped to think about it, his memories got fuzzy and disjointed. Usually, he dismissed these memory lapses as part of getting older, but more and more lately that excuse was wearing thin. And then came the headaches. The more he pushed, the more he tried to remember, the faster the headaches clamped down.

He could feel a massive headache stalking him even now. He looked up as the door opened and two men stepped in. Frank watched the men as they stood in the open door. The way they were dressed, just for a second, he thought they were an answer to his wish. But they weren't a jazz duo coming to play his bar, though he wasn't sure what they were. They looked like musicians, sort of. Both were very tall, almost freakishly so. Both were dressed all in black, black suits and large-brimmed black hats. They looked around the mostly empty room with broad smiles splitting their faces. They surveyed the room until they saw Frank. Their faces locked on him and immediately walked toward him.

"Shit," Frank said under his breath. He didn't know what they wanted, but he had a feeling it wasn't going to be good.

"Frank, my name is Mr. October, and this is Mr. July." one of the tall men said.

Frank started to smile at the ridiculous names, then the headache that had been hovering at the edge of his brain raced forward and stomped on his brain. His vision narrowed, blackness circling at the edges of his sight. Through a narrowing tunnel of dark, he saw the two men step up to him. He could see they were speaking words he could not hear through the roar that filled his ears.

After a second or a thousand years, they turned and left. Mercifully, the headache receded as they walked away from him. Frank leaned against the bar, his hands shaking. Eyes closed, he rubbed his face, pressing his fingers against his temples. On the floor at his feet was his small black notebook. He reached down and retrieved it. The door opened and his first reservation strolled in. Pushing back his queasiness, he went to work.

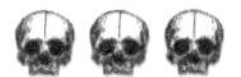

5 CAT SCRATCH DINER

Frank was in the zone. He had this routine down. He should. Every Friday for six years it was the same. Nearly a thousand eggs to be cracked, just under fifty pounds of potatoes to be cut for hash browns and bacon. He didn't even know how much bacon he had cooked. He went home smelling of it.

He moved with fluid, easy movements that got the job done. Three eggs in each hand. Crack, crack, crack, pitch to the basket, crack, crack, crack, pitch. The beer pitcher in front of him filled quickly with eggs. He emptied it into the pail at his feet and continued. These would be blended for scrambled eggs to be put in the quesadillas, a breakfast sandwich, and to be put in the pancake batter. All this work for something he thought was silly. Even the name was silly. Brunch. Who thought that up? Just a marketing concept to get people to come for breakfast. It brought in customers and that he didn't think was so silly.

He hardly watched what he was doing. His mind was running down a checklist of everything he needed. The new server was chopping red peppers and onions. She knew her way around a knife. Maybe she will work out. She seemed too young, but he felt old.

Frank stopped shelling eggs and looked at his diner. He loved every inch of it but lately he felt more tired than usual. With a sign, he tried to remember what he still had to prep.

His vision blurred slightly, which told him one of his headaches was coming on. For as long as he could remember, he had had these head splitting headaches. They always started the same way. His vision would shift almost like he was seeing two scenes at once. Sometimes he swore he could see a different restaurant than the one he was standing in. Twice, the vision was so sharp he no longer could see his own cafe. The last few months, they had gotten worse. He had seen several specialists, and none could give him a definitive answer about his headaches. One had become fascinated by his visions, attempting to document what Frank saw. Together, they had identified what seemed like five different locales of his visions. Each distinct and consistent. The specialist, Doctor Walters, thought they might be memories from Frank's past

or even past lives. As soon as the doc said that Frank laughed
and stopped seeing him.

'What malarky. 'Past lives', what BS."

Now as the diner he knew and loved faded and the vision
of a rough biker bar replaced it, he started to think he would
go back to Doctor Walters. He obviously needed help.

He stood still, looking at the bar. He knew it from past
headaches, but this time it was sharper, clearer. He could see
people moving around, hear the music and the laughter. Then
a young woman stepped up to him, frowning, "Frank? You ok
Hun?" Then she touched his arm and he leaped back.

He was standing in his cafe with the new server looking
at him, a puzzled, slightly worried look on her face.

"Ya… ya, sorry," shakily, he smiled at her, "can you finish
up here? I'll be back in a sec."

Frank pulled his apron off, draped it on a metal shelf
and pushed out into the alley. Rubbing his face, he paced the
grimy, garbage strewn alley. His breathing slowed, and the
headache slid back to sit on the horizon of his brain as he
paced in a tight circle.

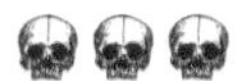

6 SCRATCH IN TIME

Frank strolled down the street, enjoying the early sun
that threw cobalt-tinged shadows across the road. He loved
this part of his day almost as much as he loved his cafe. As he
thought this, the thoughts that had plagued him for the last
several weeks returned. Somehow, someway, it was all going

to end. It was too good to last. The mood was broken. With a leadened heart, he unlocked his café and went inside.

Amongst the tables, with their up-turned chairs, the two men stood shoulder to shoulder already inside, waiting for him.

"Good morning, Frank. Is it not a splendid day?" Mr. August asked with his unnerving toothy smile. Mr. November nodded, smiling beside him. Frank, standing in the open door, just stared, mouth open, keys still in his hand.

"I… how did you get in here?"

"That's not really very important. Frank, we're here to tell you some excellent news."

Frank doubled over as a pain in his head crashed down on him, a heavy wet blanket of pain. He vomited violently, spewing across the floor, narrowly missing the two men in black.

They smiled down at him, glanced briefly at each other, then stepped forward.

Frank knew they were talking, but through his pain, he could not understand what they were saying. He panted down on all fours. His eyes squeezed shut. His spine ached.

Frank flopped sideways onto the floor, pulling his knees up and passed out. When he opened his eyes, he was alone, and the pain was gone. He stood, feeling frail and weak. On shaky legs he looked around.

A feeling of terrible loss gripped his heart. He looked at the photos on the wall of Scratch. He missed his cat for sure, always would, but this was something else. This was a loss he could not define. He knew deep inside he had lost something, but what it was, he didn't know then a flash and he remembered Scratch's purr. It flooded into his mind, washing over him. He dropped into one of the big armchairs and looked at the street as it woke. Remembering Scratch. He had so many memories. By the time the first early customer stepped up to his door, he felt better.

He rose and opened the door, placed his sandwich board out front and walked in to take his order.

Behind the counter, he looked around at his cafe. Yes, there was something, a distant pain, but this was his, and he loved it.

7 SCRATCHING OUT A LIVING

'Hell Night', two weeks later, and Frank was setting up the machine of his torture. He had already swallowed two Advils, and his stomach was in knots. The door opened, letting the street noise briefly in.

Turning, Frank started to say, "We're not open yet." He stopped when he saw the two men from before, walk in. They had on their black hats and slim suits. They smiled at Frank when they saw him. Frank's headache worsened as they walked towards him. The closer they got, the harder it became to think, to even see.

They stood in front of him. He squinted back. His head was pounding. Ripples around the edges of his vision made it hard to see. They were talking; he could see their mouths move. He could hear their voices, but he couldn't understand what they were saying. The rippling quickened, and nausea settled down on him. He was going to throw up. He bent forward, clutching his head, hand on his stomach.

The pain vanished. He was looking at the floor, sure he was about to vomit, and the pain just stopped. He straightened, puzzled and confused. The pills had never worked this well.

He searched for his headache. It was gone. He frowned at the two men standing, smiling at him.

"Thank you for your payment." Mr. July said, "Have a wonderful day." in unison, the men turned and walked out of the bar. Frank stood watching them go. Payment?

The door opened again, and a group of four walked in, laughing. He overheard one of them say something about the entire office coming by this evening for a sing-off. Frank smiled. It was going to be a busy night.

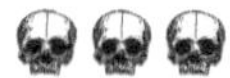

8 OL' TOM'S BACKROOM

A couple of weeks went by, and Frank had forgotten about the odd men in suits. It had been ten unbelievable days. He had received an email that said he was being sued for sexual harassment. He thought he could just laugh it off then he had spoken to a lawyer and was shocked to hear he could lose the restaurant. Just the thought of it was enough to send him into a panic. This was his place. It was the only thing he cared about. How could patting some young thing's ass mean he could lose it? It wasn't fair. He hadn't meant anything by it.

"She should be flattered, not get all uppity." He thought bitterly remembering her scowl when he had touched her.

He was at the flat top when the street door opened. He glanced over his shoulder, hoping it wasn't more bad news. He had had all he could take right now.

The two odd men walked in, smiling. A thought ran through Frank's mind. They were here that night when he brushed that girl's backside. Maybe they were working for her? He growled at his paranoia.

"What do you want?" he leaned forward, threatening.

The two men did not notice

"My name is Mr. September, and this is Mr. December."

"Wait, your names were Mr. July, and Mr. January last time. What gives?"

Their smiles seem to dim slightly, then redoubled.

"No, I am Mr. September, and this is Mr. December."

Frank straightened, crossing his arms, readying to call bullshit and throw them out when the PA system barked loud and sharp as someone plugged in a patch cord without switching off or turning the volume down. Then the room was filled with wild electric gymnastics. Whoever it was on the electric guitar, they were pretty good, but it was loud and now wasn't the time. Frank uncrossed his arms, intending to go and find out who in hell was making all the racket when he noticed Mr. September or whoever was talking. Frank stared at the smiling mouth concentrating on the lips, but he couldn't understand what was being said.

It was maddening. He wanted to throw these fuckers out, and he wanted to put a stop to shredding. He couldn't do both.

"I can't hear you!" He screamed, just as guitar lashing stopped. In the silent void, his voice boomed.

"That's not a problem, Frank," Mr. September smiled. "We are here only to thank you. Your payment has been received."

"Payment? I never paid you a dime."

"Enjoy the restaurant. I'm confident your current challenges will pass. O'l Tom will be in touch. Have a wonderful day."

Frank stared after them, wondering what that had all meant. Cursing, he turned to the flat top and his burnt burgers.

9 SCRATCHING POST

The restaurant was full, even the private dining rooms. Frank raced about, his little black book in his pocket forgotten in the heat of the night. He barely noticed when two men stepped in the front door. He glanced up as a table's orders were coming out. He wanted to check each and every order to make sure they were absolutely correct. He checked his wristwatch. He had no reservations until the turnover at 8, so these men were walkins, which was fine, but tonight he had no time for them. He dismissed them from his mind. A light tap on his shoulder made him flinch.

"Sir?" the small voice of one of his young servers quivered as he spoke. Frank glared, fire in his eyes and a harsh tongue lashing on his lips, ready to be unleashed. The young man, maybe no older than seventeen, withered under his glare. He loved the power, his power to ram his will down on the lowly staff. His pleasure vanished when he saw the two men standing behind the young man. Both towered over the server whose crisp white shirt stood out starkly against their back suits. They were smiling under their broad-brimmed hats.

Frank braced himself for the enviable headache that did not come.

"I am Mr. December, and my colleague is Mr. August." the one off to the right beamed. Out of the corner of his eye, he noticed the server scuttle away.

"Mr. August?" Frank frowned. "I..wasn't your names Mr. October or Mr. July or something last time?"

Mr. December's smile shifted ever so slightly, then it returned brighter than ever. "We are so glad you have renewed with us. Your new contract has been upgraded with a revised Clause 666."

"A revised...what?

"Yes, a revised 666 Clause. It is quite rare that head office grants a 666 revision." Mr. December's smile nearly glowed.

Frank stared at him, not understanding.

Mr. August said, "We are very happy to offer you this adjustment. Have a wonderful evening." The two spider-like men turned as one and walked out of his restaurant. Frank watched their backs recede, uncomprehending, but realising for the first time he was not on the edge of being crippled by an overwhelming headache. He didn't marvel at it for more than a second. Out of the corner of his eye, he saw that same young server about to deliver a dessert that was all wrong. He matched up behind him and placed his hand carefully on his shoulder.

10 CAT SCRATCH DINER

It was early, not even nine, but people were already lining up. Frank smiled. It was going to be a good Saturday. Maybe break his record of 180 in one day. Now, wouldn't that be great?

He strolled into the kitchen smiling, ready for a long day. He tied his apron on and happened to glance out into the empty diner. It wasn't empty. Two men stood side by side, looking at him. Frank felt the hairs on the back of his neck prickle as panic climbed up his spine.

"Good morning, Frank. We would like to speak with you." said one of the men.

"I...I..Who are you?" Frank began moving toward them even though he wanted to run out of the kitchen, out of the diner and away. His headache came back, heavy, and black. It slammed down on him. His eyes rattled in their sockets, making vision vibrate. It seemed the shift from bar, restaurant, diner and back to cafe, over and over again, but the two men in their black suits and large hats never shifted. They stood waiting with big gleaming smiles on their faces as they spoke. He could see their lips move around their large teeth, but he could only hear an occasional word.

Something about 'payment'. Frank concentrated on the men's lips, trying to decipher what was being said, then they stopped talking, their smiles seemed to broaden, then they turned and left. Frank watched their backs as they walked away. The headache backed off to perch on the horizon of his mind, waiting to pounce. Frank clutched at the edge of a table, trying desperately to calm heart. Slowly, he pushed unsteadily to his feet. The headache, a distant dark stain, slowly passed from his mind completely. He felt a calm he hadn't experienced ever in his life, a rightness as though the world had found a rare equilibrium that Frank was a part of. He rubbed his eyes, testing for his constant, painful companion. It was truly gone.

As he tried his apron on, he started thinking about a new menu. The sun was bright and warm on his patio. Brunch would soon be in full swing. He had eggs to prepare. This was going to be a great Saturday.

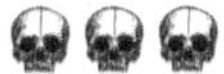

11 O'L SCRATCH TAVERN

In the dark of his room, the blanket over his window burned red gold. Frank opened his eyes and squinted at the fine hotline that edged the blanket. He rubbed his eyes and looked at his watch. Almost five. He frowned. He had slept in. He was nearly an hour late.

He untangled himself from the blanket. Shelby growled beside him. He sat, head in hands. His head ached. He rubbed his eyes. He needed a glass of water and a pot of coffee. He stood, swayed, steadied himself against the wall, and stumbled to the bathroom. The sunlight blinded him when he opened the door. For the hundredth time, he wished he had closed the bathroom curtain.

He stepped up to the toilet and pissed without aiming.

He leaned on the sink, his head deep between his shoulder blades as a wave of nausea rolled over him. It passed. He looked at himself in the mirror, squinting at the brightness. His eyes set deep, dark, ringed, vibrating with intensity. He threw up violently, mostly hitting the toilet. He knelt, his face against the cool of the toilet bowl. It was several moments before he felt he could stand. He brushed his teeth and went to the bedroom to dress.

Shelby grunted as he sat on the edge of the bed. He reached over and pulled back the cover, exposing her bare ass. It was a fine ass, he thought, lust pushing his hangover back a fraction. He reached over and grabbed her left cheek.

"Fuck off," she said as he gave her cheek a hard squeeze.

He sighed, pulled his jeans, t-shirt, and boots on, and sat for a minute longer. He looked at Shelby's ass. With a grunt, he stood and left.

His want would wait till later. Maybe a quickie in the backroom later tonight. Shelby was usually up for it if no one had pissed her off. They had been together going on six years, and it was good, better than good.

The sun was low when he stepped out. It was still too fucking bright. Squinting, his eyes like mear slits as he walked, his boot laces dragging through the gravel as he walked around to his tavern. It still gave him a thrill to think about that. 'His tavern.'

The Ol' Scratch was his, and he loved it. It was his world, and he commanded it.

Before he entered, he looked up at his fanfuckingtastic sign. Nearly eight feet high in neon, the devil with a pitchfork and a spiked tail leaned over a cowering girl in a bikini. It was nearly perfect. The only thing he would do differently was make the chick's tits bigger and probably ditch the bikini. He didn't want it in the first place, but the sign company's designer said it would make the place look like a strip club.

"An, what's so bad about that?" Frank said to the air. He pushed through the metal door. As soon as the door opened into his bar, he was fucking pissed.

He marched to where Brandi sat, making roll-ups.

"What'n'hell are ya playin'?" he hollered. They knew that he had a very strict rule about what music could be played in the bar.

Brandi ignored him, but Cayenne, halfway across the bar, flinched and dropped her tray.

"It's called music, Frank. When ya gonna join us here in the 20th century?" Brandi looked up and smiled. She knew Frank couldn't stay mad at her if she smiled.

"Music. There hasn't been a fucking song worth listening to since 1980." He growled. "Well… put on what you're supposed to be playing." He looked at Cayenne.

"'Cayenne' that's a stripper's name." Frank thought. He could not believe her parents would have given her a stripper name. Who would do that, and it really was her name. She had a driver's licence with it then again it could be fake. He still wasn't sure about her. She was too skittish, like maybe she was running from something. Maybe it was just that name that made her afraid of her own shadows. He watched her setting tables. She was cute. Not his type but good looking for sure but could she hack it. Well tonight would be a good test for her. It was wing night, and it would be busy. As he watched her, he wondered if he should have called in another girl.

He looked around the bar and glanced at his watch. Still, half an hour till the first customers showed. He could make a call. Donna would come in, or he could get Shelby off her ass and get her to help out.

"Ya that's the ticket." he said to himself. He shrugged. He'd let her sleep a bit more before rousting her out of bed.

Frank went back to the kitchen. He smiled to see Mr. Samuel. He was on top of it as usual. Frank wished he could clone Mr. Samuel. The kitchen ran so well when he was working it.

An hour later, the first wave filled the bar with loud voices, laughter, and music. Frank was behind the bar filling pitchers of beer. Brandi and Cayenne were nearly running, taking orders. Mr. Samuel was still on top, pumping out the food and the orders were coming out on time. They would get behind as the night wore on, but it would be fine.

Shelby walked in grumpy, but ready to lend a hand. He gave her a wave and a quick smile. She gave him the finger, then flashed him a smile and went to the door to greet a foursome as they entered.

It was nearing 10 when Jacob and a few of the Jurors walked in. Frank knew they would be coming. Jacob never missed wing night. Jacob was the leader of the Jurors, a local biker club. Frank heard their bikes outside and had got Brandi to set up a couple of tables for them in their corner. Frank scanned the bar to satisfy himself there weren't any yahoos looking to challenge Jacob. He was always amazed that there were still some dumb fucks that felt they could take on Jacob and not get a whooping. He didn't give a rat shit about them, but Jacob loved to break shit up using their heads, and that cost money.

Frank nodded to Shelby. He needed a smoke. She nodded back, and she took up his spot behind the bat as Frank walked out into the parking lot. Under the buzz from his neon sign, and the full roar coming through the walls of his bar, he walked around the half-full parking lot and listened to the night sounds as he pulled on his smoke.

He couldn't shake the feeling something was off, something was wrong. It should be busier, but that wasn't it. He felt like there was something he had forgotten.

"It'll pick up," he told himself. He was at the far end of the parking lot, staring into the dark. He took a drag, then flicked the butt in the trees that lined the lot. Absently, he watched the red dot arc into the dark. He turned and started walking back, his boats crunching on the gravel as a long black car slowed and turned off 11. He watched it roll slowly through the lot park, and he heard the engine shut off.

He walked up to the steps of the bar. Out of the corner of his eye, he saw the car doors open, and two men stood. A quick glance showing him two tall thin men with large flat-brimmed hats, then he was through the door and into the bar.

The look on Shelby's face told him there was trouble. He scanned the bar. "Fuck." he had been wrong. There was a young buck facing off with Jacob. Jacob was still seated, his head down, not looking at the fool standing over him.

The Jurors were sitting back, ready to watch the entertainment, big grins on their faces.

Frank forgot about the men in the car, hoping to get to the kid before Jacob decided to put him down. Then the kid said what he shouldn't have said.

"Common old man, you ain't that tough," he said. He would have said more, but Jacob came off the chair and decked him with a solid uppercut. The kid lifted off the ground, arched backward, and was out cold before he hit the ground. Jacob hadn't spilled his beer. Frank stopped. The bar noise slowly returned. The kid's friends picked him up. He staggered to his feet, with his friends holding him.

Frank was relieved. Jacob must be in a good mood. Frank watched the big man sit back down. His long beard could not cover the grin. Jacob pushed his cap back and lifted his beer in salute to the kid.

Frank watched the kid and his friends. They opened the door and stepped out just as the two men from the parking lot stepped in. They paused just inside the door, standing side by side looking at the bar. They were nearly identical, tall, and very thin, dressed in black suits. Their large-brimmed hats masked their eyes. They were smiling, and Frank knew who they were.

The bar went silent except for the loud, thin music coming from the jukebox. Jacob and the Jurors stood like a pack of wolves braced for an attack. They, too, knew who these men were.

Jacob caught Frank's eyes. Frank glanced at Jacob as he walked toward the two men. They met Frank halfway across the bar floor and stood talking. The entire bar watched, holding their collective breath. Jacob, followed by the Jurors, took a step forward.

Frank waved to them to stay, gave them a smile, but he looked scared. The two men followed Frank to the back of the bar opposite the toilets where Frank had his office. It wasn't so much of an office, more of a storage area that had a desk in it. Frank opened the door. The two smiling men ducked to enter. Frank followed and closed the door behind him. Jacob stood in the bar, watching the closed door.

After a few moments, Frank came out, pale and shaken. His eyes darted around like a small, trapped animal. They stopped suddenly, caught by Jacob's steel blue glare.

"What'd those fuckers want?" Jacob asked.

Frank glanced behind him at the door, then back to Jacob, "I...I..they....my contract..my contract is expiring," he said, staring at Jacob, fear and doubt warring in his eyes.

"The fuck," Jacob said. "What did they say, exactly?"

"Umm," Frank looked at the floor, trying to remember, "six years, six days and six hours. Ah got three days left."

"Never heard of the smiling shits ever cummin' with a warning."

Frank's eyes flashed up. He stared hard into Jacob's. He looked down and walked past Jacob. Jacob watched his back as he walked away. Jacob returned to his table, gesturing to the Jurors to do the same.

Slowly, the bar returned to normal, and Frank with it. He moved through the rest of the night as if nothing was different.

Jacob's eyes never left Frank. This was the Judge's shit, and he was an expert. He wasn't sure what exactly Frank's deal was, but it had something to do with the bar. There had been talk for many years that Frank's deal was unusual, but what that meant, Jacob wasn't sure.

Behind the bar, Shelby and Frank were talking. Jacob knew Shelby wasn't marked but knew all about it and Frank's deal. He could imagine their conversation. It was a difficult one, made only slightly easier that they both knew the score. They both knew that there was no alternative, no way out. The deal was the deal. Once made, the only release was death, and even then, you just went to Hell, where things would get really interesting.

Jacob watched as Shelby's arms flew around as she yelled, her face reddening. From where he sat, he couldn't hear what she was saying, but he could guess. Frank wasn't saying much. His head was down, and he leaned against the counter. Jacob felt his pain. Frank had made his deal and, like everyone that shook that cold hand, had been sure that the day would not come, that somehow, he would find a way out of the contract before it expired. No one ever had. Jacob knew firsthand that. His contract was non-standard and did not have the 666 clause, but he had many friends that were not as lucky and were either dead or were counting down the days till the clause came into effect, and they went to Hell.

The bar wasn't as lively as it normally was. This was Frank's bar, but it was more than that. It was Frank, and Frank was the O'l Scratch Tavern. They were inexorably tied, with Frank's energy down. So was the bar's. By closing time, only a couple of die-hard drinkers and the Jurors remained. Frank led the drinkers out into the early morning, locked up and sat with Shelby and the Jurors.

Jacob watched Frank carefully, watched his eyes. There was something he wasn't saying. He knew little about his deal.

Clyde had said there were some unusual strings wrapped around Frank, but he didn't know what they were.

"Frank. Cut the shit!" Jacob leaned forward, his voice slicing through the quiet conversation. Frank's eyes flashed up.

"Fuck you, Jacob. What do you know about anything?" Frank cowered as soon as he spoke. The Jurors tensed. They all had seen how quickly and how easily Jacob crushed men who disrespected him, but Jacob just sat back and waited. Frank stuttered, then stopped, looking around at the tense faces. Even Shelby was holding her breath.

"I...I mean…," Frank stumbled, "I…."

"What did they say?" Jacob asked, his voice calm and clear.

Frank stared at him for a long time, then he broke. He slumped in his chair, his head dipping. He looked at Shelby. She looked back at him, love and a question in her eyes. He forced a smile and gave her hand a squeeze.

"My contract is a fucking mess. I just wanted a bar. A place I could have a party every night for my friends. A place to come to for a good time, a drink or two and some good food." he looked around at the faces that were his friends, "but I didn't have a clear idea what it would look like. Not really.

Jacob leaned forward. "What's the twist?"

"The twist?" Frank's voice dripped with bitterness. "The Judge gave me what I wanted. The fucking bastard gave it all to me."

"What do you mean, 'all?'"

"Every idea for a bar, restaurant, cafe I had ever had just fell into my lap. I got them all, and he uses them to recruit. I work for him."

Jacob frowned, still not getting it.

"I have six bars, well, they're not all bars, a couple of cafes, a couple of restaurants and I run them all." Frank paused, gently pulling his hand from Shelby's. "He split me into six pieces and I am aware of all six of me going about their day."

"What did the smileys' say?" Jacob asked.

Frank stared at Jacob. "They said my contract is expiring," he glanced sideways at Shelby, "They said I could renew my contract."

"Renew your contract? That's not possible." Jacob said, his voice strained.

"Hell, I don't know. That's what they said."

"Frank, for fuck' sake. What did they fucking say?" Jacob slammed his hand down on the table, making the glasses bounce, spilling beer.

Frank recoiled. He couldn't look into Jacob's blazing eyes.

"I'm tired," Frank said quietly. "I'm so fucking tired. I can't do it anymore. It's been so hard, ya know." He looked up and met Jacob's eyes. "It's so hard being in six places at once. Thinking six thoughts, doing and saying six things all at the same time." Shelby reached over and held Frank's shoulder.

"I just can't." there were tears in his eyes. "I just can't. The price is too high." He looked at Shelby, smiled, then looked at Jacob. "The price is too high."

Jacob stared into Frank's eyes and knew. "You paid it." Jacob said under his breath, "you already paid it. Frank, haven't you?"

Frank heard but did not look up; he stared at his hands for a long time.

The door to the bar opened, and the two men in black suits and large-brimmed hats walked in.

They walked across the bar and, smiling, stopped in beside Shelby. Mr. June extended his hand to her as if he were asking her to dance. She looked at him, puzzled, then at Frank. "What's going on? Frank, what does he want?"

Frank continued to stare at his hands.

"Frank?"

Mr. June took Shelby's hand, and she stood. The other black-hatted man took her other hand, and they began walking her from the bar.

"Frank?" her voice rose in panic.

"What's going on, Frank?" Jacob asked, even though he suspected.

"Frank?" Shelby called.

Frank studied his hands. The Jurors had stood, all except Jacob. They were ready to move if Jacob said. He looked at Frank. The payment wasn't too high after all. He nodded to the Jurors to sit.

"Frank. Help Me!" Shelby fought as the men pulled her from the bar into the night. The steel door slammed shut, cutting off her screams.

A COLD HAND

Forty minutes later, he stopped, and stood still in the middle of the pavement, head down, panting.

2

OUT OF ROAD

"It's going to be fine, my love. It's all going to be fine. Don't worry, my love. It's going to be fine."

He pushed his chin deeper into his scarf, rolled his shoulders forward against the cold, and cursed as the icy claws dug into his ribs. Trying not to think about what he had left, he stumbled forward. He failed.

The cold slid inside him, past his coat, past his thin shirt, past his skin to gnaw at him. Soon he knew he would start to feel warm. That would be a lie that would lead him to believe he was fine. He wasn't sure how far he would have to go. He had driven this strip of back road many times and knew some farmers lived scattered along the road. There were long stretches where no one lived. He hoped he was close to a farmer that he could wake. Maybe a farmer that had a fire and would offer him a scotch. Which would it be? Freezing on this lonely road or a scotch by a fire. He pulled his head deeper down and walked faster. He wanted that scotch. He wanted that fire, but he definitely wanted that scotch.

The dark made the cold deeper, almost malicious, as if it wished him harm. It seemed to stalk him, a giant black beast, claws out with its prey in its sight. Even the air conspired against him. It smelled raw and blank. It burned the tip of his nose, his cheeks, and his fingertips. He looked down, concentrating on his boots. Each step crunched on the frozen gravel. He put one foot in front of the other, trying desperately to ignore the cold. His jaw hurt from clenching. Tears froze on his cheeks. No longer feeling the cuts on his face that had bled so much, nor the scratches in his palms, he winced with each step. He knew there was something wrong with his leg, but he ignored it, hoping the cold would lessen the pain for the time being.

The tips of his ears had burned for a while, but now he could no longer feel them. Nor could he feel his nose, cheeks, or his fingertips. He had wrapped his scarf around his neck and head, but the cold was unstoppable. It crawled in through his clothes with teeth. He felt the bite, pulled his arms tighter around himself, and walked.

In the distance, he saw the light of the window of the farmhouse reflecting an inviting warmth on the snow-crusted field. It would be shorter to cross the field as the crow flew, but he knew he wouldn't make it. The snow was deep, well up to his waist. It was crusted over, and he may be able to walk on the surface, but he would fall through at least every third step. He would play out halfway there.

He looked longingly at the weak yellow rectangle that was the back window of the farmhouse and wished he were there.

"Wishing ain't going ta git it done," he said with a smile, Gabriel's voice in his head. He set his teeth and forced himself to keep walking down the road. Each step scuffed gravel and kicked through the small drifts that fingered across the road almost as if they reached for him trying to trip him.

He stumbled again, falling to all fours, scraping his palms. He stayed that way for several minutes. Sitting back on his heels, he looked at the house.

'It wasn't far now, but if he stayed where he was, it might as well be on the moon.' He thought and smiled at his little joke. He looked at the moon that sat on the western horizon in an otherwise black sky. It's cold radiance made him shiver. With an effort, he stood and started walking again.

A few paces more, and he stumbled again, this time smashing down, his hands unable to catch him, and he felt the gravel and ice cut into his cheek. He lay feeling the hard road radiating cold. With an effort, he rolled onto his back. His toes had stopped burning. Now they were just dead. He remembered a movie, an old western. A horse "had gone lame," and they had to "put it down." They had shot it. He thought now that he was lame, he might have to be put down.

Once more, he forced himself upright. No longer feeling the steps he took. He willed himself to keep moving. Reaching the laneway, he turned from the road. So close now. The snow was deeper. His balance was gone, walking on dead feet. Forcing himself forward, he didn't notice the scarf had slipped. Absently, he thought that it really wasn't that cold.

He barely felt the pain when he fell forward, scraping his face once again. He was unable to catch himself. He rolled over onto his back. He struggled to stand but couldn't find the strength to push himself up. He lay back on the gravel lane with a small stone pressing into his back. It hurt. How could it hurt when he was going to freeze to death? The pebble digging into his back became his only thought and finally became his last thought.

A couple of hours later, the sun rose and shone down on his white, open, unseeing eyes. The farmer stepped out of his house, his breath billowing around his head, ready to do his morning chores. He couldn't understand what the dark shape half-covered in drifts of snow on his porch steps was. When he did, he knew he was far too late to help. He went back inside and dialled Avery. He was the local police and would need to come over and figure out who this fella had been and why he was on his doorstep.

***

The dashboard wash made his face a ghoulish mask. He scowled at the road. A small part of him regretted his haste leaving the city. His panic had overwhelmed him when he realised what day it was. He had clipped a parked car as he left the driveway. The remaining headlight lit the white lines on the highway as they flashed past and reflected in his eyes. His foot was pressed hard against the floor. Both hands held tight to the wheel as the car floated over the blacktop, engine screaming. The needle of the speedometer had wrapped the gauge and was bouncing on the pin that marked 120 mph. No telling how fast he was as he split the night air. He could feel the car's tires tentative grip on the road. He was right there on the ragged edge, at the very limit of what this car was capable of. And it wasn't enough. He was going to be late. He couldn't be late.

The white lines blurred through the tears that began flooding his eyes. He leaned his head slightly matching a curve in the road, his fingers joints creaked as his grip tightened, wringing the steering wheel. He came out of the corner and pressed harder on the gas pedal even though he knew he was running flat out. The road ahead was straight; the lines on the road disappearing ahead of him into the dark.

He glanced to the passenger seat, then to the back seat. He was alone. He felt the emptiness as a presence that hovered. His neck tingled; the hairs stood on end.

He rubbed his eyes, pressing hard, then began screaming in the purest form of rage and frustration that he had ever felt. He pounded open-handed on the steering wheel.

His grip on the steering wheel tightened. Rocking back and forth violently, he stomped on the gas pedal, wanting, needing more speed, but there was none to be had.

Six years ago, he had made his biggest deal, and walked away. He had promised himself he would never return. It was the scene of the crime, and he would never revisit it, but now his time was running out, and he had to return, return and make a new deal.

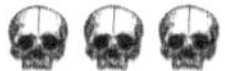

Chris looked across the lawn, regretting the last-minute decision he had made to come to this party. He looked around at the gathered crowd and couldn't understand how he fit. Were these really his peer group? Were they really his peeps? How could that be? He didn't respect anyone here. They were all dumb as fuck. With drinks in their hands, they looked so incredibly obtuse, foolish, and juvenile. The glass in his hand was empty. That was the sign. Two drinks, and he could leave. He looked around, trying to decide if there was anyone he had to say 'goodnight' to, or was it 'good afternoon.' He wasn't sure. It was sometime right between afternoon and evening.

After a minute, he decided there was no one he needed to say anything to. In fact, he did not think any of them even deserved that courtesy. He put his glass on the first flat surface he found and started walking to the door.

Then the door opened, the sunlight poured in, filling the darkened space, and surrounded in gold, she walked in. He didn't know her, yet he felt he had known her forever. She reminded him of an ad for fresh farm butter, creamy and wholesome. He smiled to himself at his cliche narrative. He instantly had a story for her, and he loved it

She walked into the room, looking around for someone she knew. Her eyes fell on him, and a puzzled look crossed her face. She walked straight up to him. She stopped in front of him, looked into his eyes. "Hi. My name is Gabriel." She extended her hand. He stared into the depths of her hazel eyes. He noticed a small imperfection, a tiny line of dark brown in her left eye. That imperfection made everything else perfect.

He smiled and said, "Hi. Chris."

And with that, the party came alive for him, and he stayed. They wandered and talked.

Six months later, he met her young son, Steven. Six months after that, he asked her to marry him.

It wasn't a perfect marriage. That doesn't exist, but it was perfect in that it was an easy blend of happy moments, challenging times, and because of his work, weeks apart.

In the beginning of their marriage, they made few business trips, but about a year in, things began to change, and they began making more trips. Chris explained that his frequent trips were a result of the business expanding, but there was another reason for his frequent trips. Gabriel thought he was having an affair, but she was wrong.

The shift happened one evening. There was nothing unusual about the night, just another Tuesday. Supper was finished, the dishes put away, Steven had gone to his room to read, and Gabriel and Chris had gone to the backyard. They sat in their lawn chairs, sipping on a Spanish red, talking, and laughing.

Chris had always loved Gabriel's stories about growing up on the farm. He found the stories quaint, as if they were from a different time.

After the second glass, she started to talk about the farm, about her parents, her brother and, of course, her dog, Hadi. She loved her dog. Hadi was her constant companion. She went for walks in the fields and brush. Hadi was walking alongside her. Her words painted a picture in his mind. He lay back, closed his eyes, and stepped into her world. He felt safe, as if he were in an old black and white movie, maybe starring Jimmy Stewart.

She talked about the warm smell of the hayloft as Saturday's afternoon sun came slipping through the cracks as she read. She talked about catching frogs at the dugout and later swimming with her brother to cool off and wash off the dust of the fields. She remembered eating fresh crab apple pie with her grandmother and watching lightning bugs float above the summer grass and the taste of the cold water straight from the well. This is the world he had seen when he saw her for the first time. It was what he had fallen in love with.

He waited. He knew what was coming next. This was the part he loved most. He loved the stories of the Judge, the devil. He loved the stories of the crossroads and the deals. He knew they were just old folktales, but they were so good. A friend had once told him he would buy a lottery ticket just to have the possibility of the dream. It was a ticket to allow the mind to wander. Her stories about the devil were like that. They freed his mind to dream of what he could have if he could walk to the crossroads and make a deal for himself. He found that over the years; he had begun to think about what he would ask for. It changed over time. He refined what he would ask for. It became clearer and more nuanced each time he thought about it.

This evening, as she spun her memories out, he sensed a change. At first, the change was slight. The wash of gold reduced little by little.

"I don't think I have ever told you about my father," she said.

He opened his eyes, hearing a change in her tone. "No. I always assumed he had died when you were young," he said, leaning forward.

"Yes, well he did," she took a sip of wine. "I was young, ten or eleven, I think. I'm not absolutely sure. You see, my father was a monster," she said, voice flat. She watched Chris's face shift. "He never wanted to be a farmer, never wanted to be a father. These he saw as traps that he couldn't escape, and when he drank, he made his unhappiness, our unhappiness. With a belt or a fist, he took his pain and anger out on my mother, my little brother, and me. But then it took a darker turn, and he looked at my little brother differently." She stared into the dark, seeing the past. "One night, I woke, and my brother wasn't in his bed. In the house, I heard my mother sobbing and down the hall another noise I didn't want to hear, so I ran away."

Chris watched her, his wine glass forgotten in his hand.

"I ran from the farm. I ran as far as I could. When I couldn't run anymore, I stood on the road in the dark. It was so dark. I didn't know where I was."

She was crying quietly, tears rolling down her cheeks when she looked into his eyes.

"Suddenly, I was blinded by a massive light, and there was a roar that broke the silence. When it ended, it was quiet again. I saw a man step out of the car that had stopped inches from me. That's how I met the Judge."

"The Judge! You met the Judge? Did you make a deal? What did you ask for?"

"Yes, I made a deal."

"You did. Wow! What did you ask for?"

She leaned closer and glanced around. "Well, I shouldn't, I'll tell you but… I sold my immortal soul for…"

"What?"

"For the ability to…"

"To what?"

"To tell a great story."

He looked at her, then her lips split into a grin, and she laughed.

For a second, his eyes wide, his mouth agape, then with realisation dropped on him, "Shit. Ok, you got me." He leaned back in his chair and laughed with her, but inside, he was furious. He didn't enjoy being played. The Judge and his deals had become an obsession for him. He had almost convinced himself that the stories were true. He could never tell Gabriel the truth, but if the Judge wasn't real, it wouldn't be long till his business was bankrupt and they were broke. Worse than broke, they were in serious trouble.

The next day, he left on a business trip. He said it wouldn't be longer than a week. He kissed her, said goodbye to Steven, and drove off.

Accord was the closest village to where Gabriel's family farm had been. It was a twelve-hour drive. As he drove, he planned his meeting with the Judge. This was his last attempt. He had been driving to Accord for the last six months. Each time more desperate to find the Judge.

It was late Thursday evening when he drove into the Ol' Scratch Tavern parking lot. He had stayed here a couple of times. Frank, the owner, had a few small rooms he let out for cheap. Chris was sure that Frank knew more than he was letting on. He just had to find a way to get him to talk.

Thursdays were the best night for his purposes. It was wing night and the busiest night of the week. There would be plenty of guys to buy a couple of beers for in exchange for some info. He had been told to talk to Jacob, but he hadn't got his courage up to speak to him yet. The one time he had approached, some young buck had stepped in front of him and had taken a swing at Jacob. He missed, but Jacob hadn't. He laid the kid out cold on the bar's sawdust-covered floor. Then he returned to his game of pool. Chris hadn't seen if Jacob had made the shot or not. He had turned away and headed for the can.

Maybe tonight he could get a chance to talk with Jacob. Chris had just under a hundred dollars in his pockets, and that was it. He either found The Judge, or he returned home stiffing Frank for the room and lying to Gabriel about what was going on again.

He sat on the edge of his bed, unable to move. "This is it," he said to the empty room. Pushing his fear down, he stood, brushing his pant legs and forcing a smile onto his face. He walked out of his room, head up putting on a swagger down the hall, past the kitchen and into the bar. It was busy but not yet full. He found a table near the pool table, close to the wall. From here, he could see most of the bar and be close to where the Jurors would be. The Jurors were the local bike gang led, Chris assumed, by Jacob. He couldn't find much out about the club. There was something there, though. They were not the usual bike gang. He knew that. He was fascinated by motorbikes and bike clubs. He didn't own a bike, never had, but he had watched every documentary on the Hell's Angels he could find. He had loved watching Sons of Anarchy, even had bought a Sons of Anarchy vest. He never wore it, though, after he had heard of people getting in trouble for having a fake double rocker crest. He didn't want trouble, just thought it was all very cool.

As soon as he sat down, the server was there. It always amazed him at how efficient they were here. He had only been to one other bar that had this level of service, and that was a few years ago in the city. A place called Ol' Tom's Backroom. He had dropped in to listen to some live music with a client. He chuckled. The owner of that bar was also called Frank.

He ordered a pitcher of beer and the smallest order of wings he could, regretting spending the money, but he needed it to look right. He couldn't appear desperate.

They arrived quickly, and he ate a couple of wings. As he had been in the past, he marveled at how good the food was. He left a couple of wings untouched so the server would leave the basket and poured himself a glass of beer. The stage was set, so to speak, and he watched the crowd. He had spoken to several people in the past. Some had just taken his beer and laughed at him. Others seemed to know more than they told him. He didn't know that they all knew what he wanted and, laughing behind his back, took his beer and told him nothing. The Judge and his deals were not for outsiders. The Jurors had spoken to anyone Chris had approached, making sure that he found out nothing.

Around ten-thirty, the door opened, and several Jurors walked in. Chris perked up. They walked across the bar, laughing, and sat at their usual table. Chris watched the door. The largest man he had ever seen stepped in. The giant ducked slightly, turning sideways as he entered the room. This was Brian, one of the Jurors, and Jacob's best friend. With a big smile, he strode across the room straight up to Chris. He leaned down, still smiling.

"So yer back. Still huntin' da Judge?" Chris flinched. He didn't like people knowing his business, but tonight was different. Tonight he had to be all in. He had to do whatever he had to do.

"Yes, I am." he looked straight into Brian's eyes, concentrating on not flinching.

Brian smiled, took one of Chris's wings and said, "Good luck." he turned and, with a bellow and a laugh, joined the other Jurors.

Jacob strode through the door a few minutes later. The air in the bar changed immediately. Chris had seen this before on one of his earlier visits. That time, Chris had thought it was fear of Jacob and the Jurors. They were a bike gang, but now he had watched the reactions of the bar. He realised it wasn't fear; it was respect. The people here respected the Jurors for their stance against The Judge. The hate for The Judge was massive. He had been going at this all wrong. He couldn't just ask for their help. He had to find another way. He had to get someone to want to give him the information. He sat back and watched Jacob sit with his brothers. A round of beers arrived. Jacob and Chris' eyes locked briefly, then Jacob took a beer, raised it to him. Chris smiled and raised his beer in return, but Jacob turned back to his table.

Chris took a swallow and surveyed the bar, trying to decide who here could be conned into 'helping' him. He needed a very good story. One that would convince someone that he wasn't looking for The Judge purely for his own gain, but for a noble cause, maybe saving his child's life. Yes, that's good.

He looked about, finally settling on an old farmer seated at the bar staring into his beer. He thought his name was Allan.

Rising, he walked across the bar and sat beside Allan. Twenty minutes later, two beers down, he had had a nice conversation about children, and the challenges they bring, but no information about The Judge.

Chris returned to his table, feeling defeated. He was out of money, out of time, and there wasn't anything he could do about it.

He sat leaning forward, lost in the foam and the dregs of his beer. He barely noticed as the bar quieted and thinned out. When he noticed, he swallowed the last of his beer and resigned. He prepared to leave. He would go to his room, and in a few hours, he would sneak out of his room and drive home. He would never return. He rubbed his face. When he lowered his hand, Allan was standing in front of him.

"Kin I sit?" he asked.

"Allan? Of course, but I was just about to leave."

"I bin thinkin' bout yer situation. I'm pretty sure you lyin' bout yer little one." He had two pint glasses in his hands. He sat and pushed one across the table to Chris.

"Ya see, me and Doreen had ourselves a boy. He did what you are fixin' to do."

"I…"

"I know what it's like to want something so badly that it becomes the only thing in yer head. It burns all other thoughts till there's nothin' left." He took a deep swallow from his beer. "My boy died because of that creature. I had a powerful hate for The Judge until I realised he could make it right. He could give me and Doreen back what he had taken. So we went an' made our deal." Bitterness dripped from every word. "No matter what you ask for, no matter what you get, it will be a lie."

Jacob and several of the Jurors pulled up chairs and sat. They did not say anything, just sat watching Allan talk.

"We haven't gotten what we asked for. You can't depend on him. He will betray you and your dream. Jacob here, don't think I should tell you what you want to know. He thinks that the Judge has taken enough an' he's right. But I know when I see a man that's reached the end of his rope, maybe got just enough to hang hisself. So I have a mind to tell you. Jacob, got anything to add?"

"No, Allan. Guess I understand. An' it's not my place to tell you what fer." The chair he sat on creaked as he sat back, looking at Chris. "You better be sure. There's no going back. Once done, it's done. We all had our reasons, and not one of us would not give anything to go back to that moment."

Chris looked from face to face. Each held a sadness and a firm determination to make him understand. "I know what I am doing. I have no choice."

"You always have a choice right up til' you meet with The Judge," Jacob said. He stood, put his chair back where he had picked it up and walked from the bar, followed by the rest of the Jurors.

Allan tipped his beer back and finished it. He put the glass down and stood. With a slight shake of his head, he said, "East on eleven to eighty-nine, then south to seventy-eight. Be there just before midnight." Allan walked from the bar. He never looked back.

Chris sat in the empty bar with a full pint in front of him.

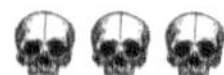

The car screamed through the night. Not that late, he could make it. He kept telling himself. Passing a semi doing well over a hundred, he wished this car had more to give.

He flew past the Ol' Scratch Tavern with its glaring neon sign. Absently, he noticed the parking lot was full. It would be a busy night.

"Oh, ya, it's Thursday," he said to the night.

Minutes later, he crested a low hill and realised he was going too fast. The turn was just ahead. He slammed down on the brake pedal. The Mustang lurched, tires howling. He was lucky as he drifted into the oncoming lane. There were no cars. When he came to a stop, he was facing the opposite direction. He shifted down to first and slipped the clutch. With a growl of some caged animal, the car hurtled forward onto eighty-nine, heading south. A quick glance at the dash told him it was eleven fifty-eight. Two minutes. He would make it. He had to.

The steering felt light, as if the car seemed to lift from the road. Gravel pinged off the undercarriage. His foot pressed hard on the floor, the wheel tight in his hands.

He lifted off the accelerator when he saw the crossroads ahead. He stomped on the brakes and drifted to a stop in the middle of the road.

He threw himself from the car, screaming. "I'm here. I'm here. I want to make a deal."

He paced, almost running around the crossroads, screaming. Forty minutes later, he stopped, and stood still in the middle of the pavement, head down, panting.

The Judge hadn't shown up. Chris had been told he never showed up twice. He thought he could convince him. He had been so sure that he would come if he really wanted him to, but he didn't. Chris sank to his knees in the dark, alone, and cried.

"Christopher. You have returned." The Judge said, his teeth, brilliant white as he leaned against his black car, his arms crossed.

Chris stammered, "Yes… Yes, I want to make another deal." He stood slowly.

"But Chris. We have a deal."

"Yes, but I want a new deal."

"A new deal? How can there be a 'new' deal? I already have your soul. What could you offer?"

"You can have all of me."

"I already have you, all of you. Come on, Chris, what do you offer?"

Chris stared at The Judge, confused. Then an idea came to him. "My son. You can have my son."

"Your son?" The Judge chuckled, "that's so ironic. If you only knew. No, not your son. After all, he's not really your son, is he?"

"No, but I offer him to you. His soul for a new deal."

"No, Chris, that would not do. You're a clever man. Try again."

"I have nothing else." he paused. "No...no, not her, not Gabriel."

"Ha, I may have been too kind. Your wife is lovely, but no, not her. No, I was thinking of someone much nicer, someone so wonderfully fresh and new. For her I would make another deal."

"No, not Laura. I won't. That will not happen."

The Judge shrugged, leaning back against his car. "That's the only deal I'm interested in."

Chris cast around the dark, looking for an answer in the shadows. He knew even as he looked, there were none. There was only one choice. What he wanted was more, more time, more success, more of what he had asked for the first time since he had made a deal. He looked at The Judge, this creature he had made a deal with all those years ago and said the only thing he could.

The drive back wasn't much slower, and without adrenaline racing through him, he drove for pleasure, letting himself enjoy the symphony of sounds that the big V8 made as he ran through the gears. The Hurst shifter snicked with satisfying precision. A small smile played on his lips as the car sucked down onto the road as it tore through the corners. This car was the culmination of a dream. When the money started rolling in, this car was one of the first things he bought. It was as close to an exact replica of the 67 Mustang GT 500 he could afford. It even had the 'Go Baby Go' button, though it wasn't connected to a nitrous tank. It was still cool. He smiled as he growled through a corner. He was heading home.

Early morning painted the landscape in shades of bluish gray. In his mirror, he could see the sky was just lightening. He rolled the window down, and the night air flooded the car, filling it with the deep earthy smells of the waking farmland. He hung his elbow out the window. The wind tugged at his sleeve. He felt at peace. The knowledge that he was going to die slid over him. It surprised and pleased him; he was not afraid. The worst thing he could think of was just days away, and there was nothing to do about it. It freed him. Like an inmate on death row, he no longer feared when he was going to die. It was nearly here, and all he had to do was decide what he would do with the remaining days.

He would spend it with his family, enjoying their company, and after he was gone, they would have wonderful memories to hold on to. Slowly, his peace was disturbed by regrets, distant regrets or small hurt that he had inflicted. He regretted his trip to the crossroads, but what he regretted most was offering his son to The Judge. He hardly had thought about it, just offered him. He resolved to make things better between them. He loved Steven, even though he wasn't his true son. He hated to admit that he felt differently toward Steven than he did toward Laura. Steven was a good kid. He was likable, and Chris did like him, but there was something. He couldn't define what it was, but there was something about Steven that made Chris feel uncomfortable. It was almost like he was hiding something or wasn't what he appeared to be. There was some underlying layer, as if he was wearing a skin that didn't quite fit him.

He shook his head and chuckled. He was being stupid. It was all in his head. He would make sure he and Steven had some solid father son memories.

The morning sun painted the blacktop golden, and blue shadows raced ahead of the Mustang as it devoured the miles.

Turned away from the snowy dark rushing past the window, Laura's head rocked as she slept in the backseat. Her eyes flashed behind her eyelids. She was dreaming of her first day at school. It had been magical, far better than she had imagined. She had been playing 'school' with her dolls and teddy bears, sitting on the floor of her room in neat rows. She had been the teacher, of course. Going to school had been completely different, but so much fun. There were so many kids to play with. Steven, her brother, had met her at recess and walked her around showing her the school, introducing her to his friends. Thinking of him made a smile play across her lips. Her dreams shifted, becoming disjointed and frightening. Something was coming, something dark and unseen. It shuffled through the hallways, coming closer. She called for her brother Steven, who was always there for her. She couldn't find him and she got worried, she looked for him in the school that looked nothing like the school she had been at earlier. Shadows crept from around corners. She ran, calling for Steven. She stumbled, a shuffling noise right behind her. She did not dare look back.

Still half in her dream, her eyes closed, she could hear her parents talking quietly. She frowned, wanting to sleep more but not wanting to be chased.

"Hey, sleepyhead," her mom said. "Why don't you sleep a bit more. We still have a way to go." she reached back and touched Laura's hand. "Go back to sleep, my sweet."

Laura smiled and nodded. She looked out at the dark. Shapes flashed past, and maybe she slept. In her dream she wasn't being chased anymore, but she couldn't find Steven. He was close, but he was hiding just out of sight. She stood on a dark highway, standing on the painted white line. In every direction, a road led away into the black that surrounded her. She shivered, alone in the night.

Chris pushed himself to all fours and coughed. His ears were ringing. He sat back on his heels, tilting his head back. The snow fell in big fat flakes. He looked up into the dark sky and watched them as they floated down. His face burned, and he had a terrible headache. He closed his eyes, swaying in the cold. His breath frosted the air. He smelled the air. It had the smell of just before a big rain storm.

He noticed a crackling, a snapping that seemed to be accompanied by bluish lightning. He could feel the crisp chill around him.

An arc flashed, illuminating the black, twisted trees, the snow-filled ditch, and the car that tilted at a troubling angle. He stared at the car for a long time, not understanding. Inside, he felt a growing need to check. The need turned urgent. He scrambled to his feet and immediately stumbled, falling forward, his palms scraping against the frozen pavement, small icy stones cutting his skin. Clawing, he got to his feet and hobbled across the blacktop to the car. Hot metal ticked as it cooled. Steam escaped from under the twisted hood, steam and maybe smoke.

Fragments of memories flashed through his mind. A scream, the hot flash in his brain, a panicked jolt as the car moved like it shouldn't, like no car could. He remembered thinking, "Not now, not yet, I can't be here. Not now!" as panic set in.

There was so much blood. It looked black against the snow like splattered India ink flicked across clean white sheets in the dark. He staggered around the car, pushed through the deep snow, and reached the front passenger door. The front of the car was mangled beyond any logical reason. A sheared power pole lay half on the road. Above the scene, bluish arcs from the damaged transformer cast wild dancing shadows on the snow.

He braced his feet against the car's side and pulled the door open. It moved only a fraction. With his bare hands, he pushed the snow back and tried again. This time, he managed to open the door enough to squeeze in. A flash of cold blue light showed him what he never wanted to see.

Gabriel lay mostly on the front seat. The inside of the car was splashed with glistening black. For a brief moment, he thought she looked like one of Laura's dolls, broken and tossed aside. Laura! He leaned past Gabriel into the back seat and could not understand the ruin he saw there.

The pole that the car had severed in half had spun them then smashed down on the car. Part of it pierced the windshield, tearing through Gabriel's arm and into the back seat where Laura slept.

What Chris saw there did not make any kind of sense. The seat was black and glistening. He stared, trying in vain to understand what he was seeing, finally deciding Laura must have been flung from the car as he had. He turned his attention to Gabriel. He couldn't see how badly injured she was. Somewhere in the tangle of wood, metal, glass, bone and flesh was the woman he loved. He leaned deeper into the wreckage and touched her face. Her eyes popped open. They flashed around wildly, the whites stark in the gloom.

"Laura? Is Laura, ok?" Her frantic eyes found his and locked.

"Yes." He said, knowing he was lying. He touched her cheek with his fingertips. He felt her shudder.

"It's going to be fine, my love. It's all going to be fine. Don't worry, my love. It's going to be fine."

The Judge walked around his car, easy and supremely in his element.

3
THE RIDE
Original published in A Single Round

The sound of air brakes was the sweetest sound he had heard in a long time.

The hitchhiker hadn't seen a car or truck for almost two hours, so when the lights of a rig topped the hill, he leaped to his feet. It had started to rain an hour ago, and he knew he had miles to go before he got to a town. The highway he was on wasn't used as much as it once had been. He was on the old highway, a two-lane blacktop that serviced the small towns and villages that had been missed when a four-lane had been put in a few years ago.

The rig slowed and bounced slightly as it pulled to a stop beside the hitchhiker.

The young hitchhiker stepped up and pulled the door open. He pushed his backpack and guitar case up in front of him. The driver was a big man with massive arms, neck, and shoulders. He took the guitar case and backpack and pushed them into the berth behind.

The hitchhiker pulled himself up into the seat. He almost groaned with relief in the warmth of the cab. He was pale, almost white, with long dark hair plastered to his head.

The driver held out his hand. "Gordon," he said.

The hitchhiker took the huge hand, shook it once and said, "Steven. Thanks for stopping."

"Almost didn't. I thought you were an animal or a pile of trash 'till you stood."

Gordon pushed the rig into gear and concentrated on getting up to speed. Once they got moving, he reached behind his seat and pulled out a roll of paper towels.

"Here, ya go. Ya, look half drown." Gordon handed the towels to Steven.

"Yeah, thanks," he said, and started drying his hair.

"Where ya headed?" Gordon asked.

After a long pause, Steven said, "Just going to meet someone."

Gordon watched the kid dry his hair. He had a haunted look, as though he had been living rough for a while. His clothes, jeans, t-shirt and a light jacket were dirty and worn. His eyes had a brightness somewhere between near-madness and fear. He was very pale.

"You bin on the road awhile?" Gordon asked.

"Yeah, couple of months," Steven said. His reflection looked back at him. Outside, the dark landscape passed by.

"My folks died in a wreck. I need to find out why." His tone was flat as if he was talking about the weather.

"I'm sorry to hear. What do you mean, find out 'why'?"

Steven looked at Gordon.

"Ah, it's nothin'. Just gotta check something."

It was quiet for a time. The kid's wet clothing gave off a slight animal smell.

"I'm gonna be making a stop in 'bout an hour." Gordon said. "It's my usual stop for some grub. Good place called The Ol' Scratch Tavern. Food's decent, better than decent. Frank flips a mean burger. It's a bit rowdy, but good folks."

"Yeah, I'm gonna be late if I don't press on."

"Yer meeting is tonight?" Gordon glanced at the dash clock. It was well past 10. The kid followed his look and frowned. It was obvious the math didn't add up.

"I guess I won't make it tonight," Steven said, more to himself than to Gordon.

"Well, in that case, let me buy you a burger."

"Naw, I got money. Let me buy you one for picking me up."

"You sure?"

"Yeah, for sure. No problem. I guess I got to find a place to crash tonight."

"Ol' Scratch rents rooms. Nuthin fancy, but clean."

"Perfect."

They were quiet for a few miles.

"Who ya meeting if ya don't mind me askin'."

Steven looked at the trucker for a long time. "Calls himself The Judge. Don't know his real name."

He watched as Gordon stared at him. Steven looked back at the road, and the pools of light the rig's headlights cast.

"Ya I heard ah him." Gordon watched the lines on the road. "It's none of my business, but it ain't a good thing ya go meetin' The Judge."

"Yeah, it's none of your business," Steven replied quietly.

Gordon shrugged. He knew that mindset. He had seen it before. People that were dead-set on seeing the Judge had that look. They weren't going to be persuaded.

After a little more than a half-hour, lights appeared in the distance. Bright pink, white and red neon washed the sky in crimson.

As they got closer, 'Ol' Scratch Tavern' could be read in huge glowing letters. And a depiction of a pointy tailed devil threatening a bikini-clad woman.

Gordon grinned. Seeing that sign, ugly as it was—told him he was going to have a good meal with good people. He glanced over at his hitchhiker.

The neon turned his pale skin a sickly red, which when mixed with the greenish dashboard lights, made him look ghastly, almost ghoulish.

The Ol' Scratch had a large gravel parking lot west of the building. Gordon geared down and rolled into the parking lot. The area closest to the blacktop had a section that was generally reserved for semis. It was open even though the rest of the parking lot was packed.

Gordon eased the rig in and shut her down. He turned to Steven.

"Coming?"

Resigned, Steven said, "Yeah, sure."

Gordon climbed down, a smile on his face. The parking lot was a good indication of what was happening in the bar.

It was going to be packed. Gordon loved it that way. After spending so many hours on the road alone, it was fantastic to be with people. Together they crunched across the gravel parking lot. It was full of mostly pickups, with a couple of tired beat down cars scattered about. The neon glinted off chrome and paint, making even the tired old cars look good.

Off to the south of the building, where the neon didn't touch, were parked a bunch of bikes. No cruisers, all customs, choppers, bobbers, mostly apes, some low-slung belly draggers, all Harleys. A few Knuckleheads, but mostly pan heads.

Steven's dad had been a rider, sort of and had owned several Harleys. He and his father had fun looking at bikes. His dad seemed to buy a new one every year, all customs. Steven always went along.

He knew this was an unusually impressive collection of bikes, and he paused to look at them. Gordon followed his eyes.

"Ya, that would be The Jurors bikes. A couple of the members are fine custom bike builders. The bobber over there is Jacob's." Gordon pointed to the right at a nice vintage-looking bike. "If you want to talk to The Judge, you should talk to Jacob. They're all marked, but Jacob is their leader if there really is a leader."

"Marked?" Steven looked back at Gordon.

"Yeah, they've all made a deal with The Judge."

Steven looked up sharply. "They've sold their souls?"

"Ya." Gordon shrugged, turned, and headed for the door. "What for?"

"Ha, who knows? Various things, but it's not like I know 'em personal like. Just know that they are marked. It's reason for the club's name. Kinda ah joke, ya know. The Jurors."

Steven caught up and grabbed the door as Gordon walked through.

The bar was loud. It staggered Steven just how loud it was. Out in the parking lot, it had been a low, consistent hum he had heard but, after riding in the semi's cab, had seemed quiet. Steven stared about the dark room. Everywhere he looked were people, mostly men, laughing, talking, shouting. There was so much movement it sort of blended into a writhing mass. He stood still, just watching when he heard over the clamour a sharp, high-pitched whistle. The sound brought him from his trance.

He looked to his right and saw Gordon waving him to follow. He moved forward, holding his guitar case in front of himself, trying not to jostle anyone. He got up behind Gordon and followed closely, moving in his wake. The big trucker made a large path through the crowd without pushing or shoving. The crowd just moved out of his way. Steven was grateful when they made it to the bar. He placed the guitar case up against the bar and pulled off his backpack, lowering it to the floor beside the case.

Gordon had found a couple of chairs not side by side, but a brief conversation got the guy sitting in one stool to move over so they could sit down elbow to elbow. They sat, Steven, looking around, still slightly mesmerized by the scene.

Gordon laughed and clapped him on the back.

"Ya it sumpin', ain't it" Gordon looked over the bar.

Jacob gripped the axe and felt it hum.

"Mostly farmers and some fellars from the plant south ah here." Gordon saw The Jurors off in a corner near the pool table. He pointed. "There's The Jurors over there."

Steven looked at where Gordon was pointing. "Holy fuck!" Steven said, looking at the biggest man he had ever seen.

Gordon laughed, "Ah ya, that's Brian. He's one big mother fucker for sure. Heard tell he sold his soul to be invincible, but it turned out everything that hurts him just makes his body compensate by getting bigger and stronger. He also gets dumber as well. Kinda ah cliché, but I guess the Judge has a sense of humour."

The bartender arrived. He was an older man with an unshaven face and a weary look in his eyes. They darted about the bar, seeming to see everything. Arms wide, his hands flat on the bar, he leaned forward and nodded.

"Hey, Frank. A couple ah beers an' a couple of yer burgers." Frank smiled and did not even try to talk over the noise.

Steven was still watching The Jurors. He leaned over to Gordon's ear,

"Which one is Jacob?"

Gordon looked at Steven with a frown and looked over the heads toward the corner. After a second, he leaned toward Steven.

"See the big guy with a big grey beard sitting over in the corner?'

"Ya."

"That's Jacob. But best ya don't bug him now. Best wait till things quiet, a bit." Gordon turned back to the bar as their beers arrived. Steven stared at Jacob. He sat leaning back against the wall, a beer in one hand, a pool cue in the other. He was a large man, lean with muscular arms. He sat with a confident, quiet stillness—a small grin playing on his lips. The ball cap he wore shaded his eyes. There was a sparse wolf quality to him.

Gordon patted Steven on his back, and he turned to the bar.

The pint looked good. Steven picked it up. They touched glasses, and Steven pulled at the beer. God, it tasted good. He hadn't had a beer or much of anything for several days. Now here and now, this beer tasted just about as good as a beer ever does. He looked at the smiling face of Gordon.

"Good?" Gordon asked.

"Damn right." Steven took another swallow. He felt himself relax more than he expected to. He looked up into the mirrors behind the bottles and watched the bar.

The Jurors kept to the corner around the pool tables. No one approached; no one even looked in their direction. Gordon was right. They all looked to Jacob as the leader, even though Jacob didn't seem to notice. He sat back, drinking his beer and enjoying himself. He had relinquished his cue. If Jacob was the leader, then Brian was his second.

Brian laughed and joked in the center of them all. A giant of a man obviously loved by them. Steven shook his head. Brian was the largest man he had ever seen. More massive than any bodybuilder or powerlifter he had ever seen on tv. He towered over them all and yet seemed almost gentle.

Steven noticed something odd. The Jurors never called the waitress over to order. She just arrived with a tray of beers. At first, he thought they had a running tab, but after every round was delivered, The Jurors all took their beers, turned to another table in the bar and raised a toast to the table. The table returned the salute.

The bar was taking turns buying the Jurors rounds. Table after table sent rounds over to them. It was respect. It wasn't fear that kept the patrons from approaching the Jurors. It was respect. The entire bar was paying tribute to the Jurors.

"Now that's interesting. So, what does the town think of the Judge?" Steven thought.

The burgers arrived. He looked down.

It did look like a good burger. It looked like a burger a close friend would que up for him on a Saturday afternoon. Big and meaty. It was called the Hades burger. Steven looked up at the chalkboard with the menu written there. Everything was named after something to do with the devil or hell. It was, Steven thought, a bit obvious.

He took a swallow of beer and started in on his burger. It was good, very good. Gordon was already nearly finished. He seemed to be really enjoying himself. The big man hunched over, elbows on the bar, both hands wrapped around the burger as he attacked it.

Steven smiled as he was looking around enjoying the surrounding cacophony. This was nice. He was right. Good food, good people.

He was halfway through his burger when he realised, mixed in with all the laughing and talking, was music, not canned music, but a band. He put his burger down and slid off the barstool and started making his way deeper into the bar. Where the long wooden bar ended, the room turned and expanded, and there was a much larger room with a stage, and a three-piece was doing its best to be a little band from Texas. They had just rolled into their version of 'La Grange', and Steven felt his face split into a grin. They were pretty good. They even had beards not as long, but still. He suddenly felt lighter than he had for weeks, months. He stood and wished he had brought his beer.

The band had finished 'La Grange' and had started 'Tush' when a voice beside him said. "I fucking love this song."

Steven looked to the sound of the voice. It was Jacob, standing beside him, smiling at the band.

"Yeah, me too. My all-time favourite band," he said suddenly, not listening, "You're Jacob."

Jacob paused, the beer almost at his lips. He took a swallow. "Ya." He looked at Steven. "And you are?"

"Ah... Steven." he stuck out his hand awkwardly.

Jacob looked at it, ignored it, and looked up. "So 'Ahsteven,' how is it that you know my name?"

"I hitched in with Gordon."

Jacob looked back to where Gordon could just be seen, burger finished and fresh beer in hand. Jacob looked back at Steven.

"I need to speak to the Judge. I need to ask him a question," Steven said. He had yelled it just as the music paused. He looked around. Everyone close enough to have heard was looking at him.

"Not something you should be yelling in a bar where you aren't known." Jacob turned and started walking away.

"Jacob I...I need.."

Jacob stopped, turned, and looked back at Steven.

Everyone near was very purposely not looking at the two men.

"You can't talk to the Judge. He's not the talkin' sort. He just takes what he wants and gives nothing back. Leave him alone. He's not the answer."

"But he killed my parents, and I want to find out why."

"He killed a lot of folks round and worse than that. He has a lot to answer for, but you're not the one." Jacob looked at the beer in his hand. "Sorry 'bout yer folks," and he turned and walked away.

Steven made to follow when a big hand fell on his shoulder.

"That's it, kid. Leave it be." Gordon said, pushing a beer into Steven's hand. "I've seen Jacob get mean."

"I'm not afraid of him." Steven was cocked up, ready to take on the world.

"Ya, well...I am," Gordon said, pulling Steven with him. "And you should be. C'mon I spoke to Frank. He has a room for you. Get yer gear, and someone will show you yer room."

"I just need him to tell me where I can find the Judge."

"Well, maybe Frank knows; he seems to know pretty much everything that's going on 'round here."

They sat down on the stools. Drinking their beer and watching the crowd. It was getting close to midnight, and the bar was starting to empty out.

Later that morning, Steven lay in the dark in his rented room. He wasn't sleeping. He was thinking. Outside his window, he heard The Jurors kick their bikes to life and rumble away into the night.

Jacob knew. Jacob knew how to talk to the Judge. He knew. Steven was sure. But he was also sure he wasn't going to tell him. All The Jurors knew, but without Jacob's OK, they wouldn't talk either.

Gordon was off making his drive. He said he would be coming back through in a day or two if Steven needed a ride out.

"Fuck it." he wasn't going to get any sleep, he thought. He pushed out of bed and flipped the light on.

He stood in the middle of the plain room, not sure what to do. He bent over and opened his guitar case. He looked down at the prize. His dad had come back with it a long time ago, right about the time his business started to take off. Now, looking back; Steven could not figure how his dad could have afforded a guitar like this. It was a Kalamazooo KG-14 flat-top guitar, and it was beautiful. Steven didn't play guitar, but he could see, even feel, this was a special guitar.

He knew about guitars just like he knew about bikes, because his dad knew about bikes and guitars. He had never ridden, nor had he ever played. Nor had his dad.

His dad had fine bikes and guitars. Many of them. He felt it gave him an air of rough-edged mystery. He thought it romantic to tell a story of rags to riches. From a guitar-playing bike riding streetwise kid to a high-powered money executive.

It was all a facade—a story he fabricated and maintained. Steven hated his dad for it. That and so much more. But he never wanted him dead. He missed his mom. She was sweet. She didn't care about all the money. She was just a farm girl who fell in love with an ambitious man.

He loved her quaint stories of growing up on the farm. It had become part of the family legend, part of the myth. She told her stories, but one caught his attention more than the others. The one about the crossroads and the Judge. He really liked that one. Asked to hear it again and again. Steven's mom laughed about it at first, then found it frustrating. It started to worry her.

Just after Steven's 12th birthday, his dad's business started to do well. Very well. He had come back from one of his many business trips. He had always gone on several trips a year. After one trip, everything changed. Suddenly things were great. They had everything they ever wanted, and Steven's mom forgot about her worries about the Judge and the crossroads. Steven's father never went on another business trip. A year later, they had a baby, and Steven had a sister.

Her name was Laura, and Steven loved her. Most of his friends hated their little sisters or little brothers. They were annoying and always around, but Steven liked Laura. She was easy and friendly. She was fun to be around. He loved being a big brother. He loved taking care of her.

When his parents needed him to sit so, they could go out, he was happy to look after her.

When Laura was 5, she started school at the same school Steven was at. He was so excited. On her first day, he walked her to school and showed her around. It was his last year, and he wanted her to feel safe. He met her at lunch and sat with her. Some of his friends from the art club sat with them and were nice to her. They talked about the yearbook they all were helping design. It was exciting.

After school, he walked her home. Their mom was waiting. Laura ran from Steven's side, telling her mom all about her day. Her mom smiled and looked at Steven.

"Thank you, Steven," she said.

"No problem. It was fun. I have to go back to the school. We're working on the yearbook with Mr. Sauvé."

"Dad was going to take us all out for dinner to celebrate Laura's first day," his mom objected.

"Ugg, I would love to, but I can't. Not tonight."

"OK. When will you be home?"

"8? Probably."

"K,"

Steven kissed his mom's cheek, patted Laura's head, smiled at her, and started walking back to school.

It was the last time he saw her alive. He missed her most of all.

The next morning, he packed his backpack and went into the bar. It looked surprisingly different. It still stunk of beer, but the tables had been moved around. There were several tables full of people eating. Some had full tables, a couple had singles.

Frank was there serving, with a couple of servers helping out.

Frank saw Steven. He lifted his chin in recognition. He gestured to an empty table. Steven nodded and walked over, setting his guitar case and backpack on the floor beside the table. He sat just as a pretty server stopped by his table.

"My name is Brandi. Coffee to start?"

Steven looked up. "Yes," he stammered, feeling like a small boy.

"Coming right up, hun." she smiled and turned to the table to Steven's right.

"The usual, Billy?"

"Yup, thanks."

"You got it, sweetie."

She walked off. Several eyes followed her every step.

Steven leaned back and looked at the chalkboard menu.

The devil theme continued. The 'hell-of-a-breakfast' looked like a shit ton of food, the 'Brimstone toast,' toast with avocado and spicy jelly. Looked more like what he needed. Devilled eggs, Purgatory poached eggs, Netherworld quesadilla, all served with a Bottomless Pit of coffee.

Steven chuckled. He looked up when Brandi put his coffee down in front of him.

"Know what you want, hun?"

"Yeah, the Brimstone toast."

"Ok, hun."

She smiled and turned to Billy.

"Just a sec on your Hella, Billy."

He nodded. Steven watched him as Brandi walked away.

Billy was staring at his phone; absently, he looked to the floor beside him. He swore, then reached down and picked up a twenty from the floor.

"Fuck," he said, then softer "fuck." He looked up and caught Steven's eyes.

"My lucky day," he said, but he didn't sound happy about it.

"That's great," Steven said.

"Just great," Billy frowned.

Brandi returned with a huge plate piled high with food. Three eggs, two pancakes, three strips of bacon, two sausages, orange juice, toast and, of course, the bottomless pit of coffee.

"That's a big breakfast," Steven said.

Billy grinned, "yup," and he dug in with gusto.

After a few minutes, Steven's food arrived. Billy looked up. "That don't look like enough breakfast."

"Yeah, it's enough."

Billy turned back to his plate. He was plowing through it in a hurry.

"Listen," Billy said. "If things er tight, I'll spring for yer breakfast. I jus found a twenty." He grinned.

"No, I'm good. Thank you, though."

Billy grunted and returned to his food. Steven thought for a second. Gordon has been right, good food, good people.

Steven ate his toast, enjoying it. The coffee was excellent, too. When he finished, he leaned back. Billy was finished as well.

"Well, 'bout time fer a nap." Billy stretched. "Where you headed?"

"Nowhere special. I got some business 'round here. After, I don't know."

Billy took a sip of coffee and looked at Steven.

"Yer not fixin' to go see The Judge, are ya?"

Steven looked at Billy, then down at his empty plate.

"What if I was?"

Billy nodded to himself as if he had known it. "Ya, you have that look."

He looked at Steven. "I'm pretty sure I can't change yer mind, but I won't sleep so good if I didn't try."

"It's not what you think. I'm not here to make a deal. I'm here to return something to the Judge. I don't want it. It wasn't my deal. It was my dad's."

"Yer dad's, eh?" Billy seemed to think for a minute.

"It don't matter. You go see him, and your life is done. It don't matter what you think you came to do. He will twist it into your worst nightmare. It's what he does." Billy shook his head.

"You seem to know a lot about this," Steven said.

"Ya well, I was a fucking fool. I made my deal, and now I'm cursed."

"So you sold your soul?"

"Ya I did." Billy looked down, embarrassed. "An fer no good reason. I wanted to be lucky. I figured it was safe, I mean, how could that turn bad. Ha, I was so wrong."

"Lucky?"

"Ya. I'm lucky, alright. The trouble is no matter what I win, someone I know gets unlucky to the same amount. It's a balance thing, I was told. I think it was just The Judge likes fucking with people." Billy's voice was heavy with bitterness.

"Well, I'm not here to make a deal. I just want an answer to a question."

"Well, I heard tell that Jacob tried damn hard to get some answers but didn't get anywhere."

"Yeah, I tried to talk to Jacob last night. He seemed less than talkative."

"Ya, Jacob ain't a talkative kinda guy. He has a serious hate on for the Judge, but he won't talk to no one. Not even me an' we're sorta friends."

Steven watched Billy. They both took a sip of coffee.

"I just need to know where to meet him."

"Look, you're not hearing me. Don't do this. It won't work. You won't get what you want."

"I need to find out why."

"Why? Why what?"

"I need to know why my sister had to die. I understand my fucking father. He was the one who made the deal. He's the one who was responsible."

"Ya, he's the one, but it may just have been bad luck."

"It wasn't. It was the deal. It had to be."

"K, what do you know about his deal?"

Steven looked at his coffee cup. It was empty.

"Not much really."

"When did he make it?"

"He went on a business trip when I was 12. He came back with this guitar." Steven pointed down at the guitar case beside him. Billy looked down at the case.

"Afterward, things changed, got better. We had money."

"When did your dad die?"

"Three months ago. It's been three months since my family died, since my sister died." Steven looked at his coffee cup. It was full.

He looked up at Billy in surprise.

"Ya, Frank made a deal to have this joint. In fact, I think there are more joints scattered about with a different version of Frank in each. Frank is always going on about his headaches. It must be a bitch to be in several places at once."

Steven looked at his full cup of coffee. He took a sip. It was great coffee.

"It's good coffee, isn't it?" Billy raised his cup and took a sip. "It's too bad that it's almost over."

"What do you mean?"

"That's what I was trying to get to. Frank's deal is a standard contract. 6 years, 6 months and 6 days. I don't know fer sure, but I'm pretty sure he's just about done."

"My sister died 6 years, and I think 6 months from when my dad went on his business trip that changed everything."

Billy nodded his head.

"So it was a standard 666 contract. Now you can work out the exact day yer dad was here and went to the crossroads. I don't know that helps much, but it's a start. I don't get the guitar though. Was yer dad, a famous guitar player?"

"No, he never played. He made his money trading."

"Trading?"

"Ya, he managed clients' money for them."

Billy had no idea what Steven was talking about. He sighed, took a swallow of his coffee.

"I'm not going to talk you oudda goin', and I ain't a hypocrite. Take 11 west for 6 miles, then turn south at the turnoff at the gas station. 6 miles exactly, you'll come to the crossroads."

"Thanks," Steven said. Billy stood. "I ain't done you no favours. I should have left ya be, but iffin' yer dad made a deal and that there guitar has sumpin' ta do with it, well shit, who knows." Billy turned and left.

Steven finished his coffee and left the Ol' Scratch. He walked out to the blacktop and started walking west. He walked for half an hour without seeing a car. He paused to look at a highway sign. It read '11.'

He continued west, and almost immediately, an old red pickup slowed and pulled up beside him.

"Where ya headed, son?" The face of the driver who peered at him through the open window was a mass of wrinkles. An old dog lay on the blanket that covered the seat.

"Morning. Thanks for stopping. I'm just heading up the road a bit to a service station."

"Well, I can take you that far fer sure. That's where I turn. Hop in."

Steven put his guitar in the back, along with his backpack. He pulled the door open and climbed into the truck.

The dog sniffed his hand, whimpered, lay its head down on its paws and went back to sleep.

"This here is Gunner."

"Hey, Gunner." Steven patted the old dog.

"Not all dat sure Gunner hears much, but he's a good ol' dog."

Gunner raised his head and looked up at the old man.

The old guy smiled and pushed the truck into gear. The truck rumbled along. The old guy was dressed in jeans and a denim shirt. He had a sweat-stained green ball-cap.

"Name's Allan."

"Steven."

"Where ya headed? Yer not from round here."

"My mother was. She grew up on a farm around here. Family name of Cooper."

"Cooper ya say. Ya, I seem to recollect some folks named Cooper farmed around here but dat was sometime back. I was jus a kid. Seems ta remember some trouble wit 'em."

"Couldn't have been my mother's family. She just passed. She was in her 40's. She left the farm probably in the 80s."

"Don't s'pose."

The fields rolled by. Steven breathed deep. The strong smell of earth filled him. It was good. The sky was clear.

"Crops er coming long nicely. Should be a good year if we git enough rain," Allan said, not really to Steven. Steven looked at the fields, not understanding what the old guy saw, but feeling content.

He realized he felt like he was home. As though he had been away for his entire life, and here he was coming home. The air smelled like home somehow. He had never been here, and something inside him quieted. A small thing that had buzzed and fluttered his entire life was quiet for the first time. He only noticed it in its absence.

"Well, here we are. I'm turnin south. It's nun of my bin'nus but would you be head dat way too?"

Steven looked at the old man and his sharp, shrewd eyes. A small grin was playing with his mouth.

"Yeah, I am," Steven said.

"Ha knew it. Yer fixin to see da Judge, ain't cha?" Allan smiled as if he had guessed a great secret.

"Yeah, I am," Steven said quietly.

"Well, it ain't my pig an' it ain't my farm bu' I think yer just batshit crazy!"

Steven laughed. "You may be right."

Allan laughed back. "Well, den I s'pose ah kin drive ya there. It's a might early. Tell ya what, let's head to my farm. My Doreen will fix us some lunch an' I'll put ya ta work fer a bit then I'll drive to the crossroads ta do yer bin'nus."

"I don't want to put you out, but that would be great."

Allan slowed and turned south. Steven saw the sign 'township road 78'. The truck bounced and hesitated and rumbled on as Allan shifted through the gears.

Gunner raised his head and sat up. He knew he was almost home. Suddenly the cab of the truck filled with a stink Steven couldn't identify. It was foul.

"Fuck Gunner, couldn't ya waited, jeez!" Allan said and laughed. Steven groaned and laughed as well. They were still laughing when Allan turned the truck off the road and pulled up beside a nice bungalow in a large farmyard. He stopped and shut the truck off in front of a garage with its door open. Past the garage was a large old red hip-roofed barn.

"C'mon."

They walked from the truck, Gunner leading up to the two-tone, small pretty house. The wooden stairs had small flower pots with pansies of various colours. It was obvious Allan and Doreen were proud of their home.

The door opened, and an enormous woman filled the doorway. She had an equally enormous smile on her face.

"Allan, what have you brought home?"

"This here is Steven. He's coming for a spot of lunch, and later I'm driving him over to have a meeting."

She looked down at Gunner, who licked her hand. Gunner lay down on a mat by the door. The woman looked back at Steven and frowned. "Well, I'm happy to feed him fer sure. No good kin come from those meetauns. No how." She stepped back, and Allan held the door for Steven.

"You don't take her no heed. I know nuthin we kin says gonna change yer mind, so that's that. Go on in."

Doreen scowled at Allan; her big smile returned as she guided Steven to the dining room.

"Here, sit here. I'm afraid it's not much. I was making grilled onion and cheese sandwiches."

"That sounds fantastic," Steven said, and meant it.

Allan came in and sat in his chair. There was a glass of water in front of him. Doreen called from the kitchen, "Drink yer water, Allan."

Allan grumbled and drank the water. Steven watched him. Allan had been a tall man, now bent over and shrunken. His fingers reminded Steven of day-old chicken wings, dry, brown and shrivelled. The skin over his knuckles was thin and had a papery look; between the knuckles, his skin was very dark, almost black.

Doreen came in and placed plates in front of Steven and Allan with two triangles of toasted bread dripping with cheese and sliced onions. They smelled wonderful. She kissed Allan on his bald head as she passed him. Allan's face was tanned dark from his neckline to just above his nose, and from there up his skin was fish white. He had a few stray white hairs on the top of his head, but mostly he was completely bald.

Doreen came in with a plate for herself.

"What can I get you to drink, Steven?"

"Water would be great thanks."

She left and returned with a glass of water for him.

Steven was about to pick up his sandwich when Doreen grabbed his hand and, grasping Allan's hand, she bent her head. Steven looked to Allan, who winked and bowed his head. Steven bowed his head and waited.

After a minute, Doreen raised her head and smiled at Steven.

"Dig in."

She picked up her sandwich and ate. Steven followed suit.

They didn't talk as they ate. It was a quiet, efficient meal. When they had finished, Doreen picked up the plates and headed back to the kitchen.

"Coffee?" she called over her shoulder.

"I would love a cup, my love," Allan said.

"Yes, that would be great," Steven said.

"Hey, Doreen. You 'member a family that farmed 'round some time back, name of Cooper?"

"What's that? Cooper?" her head came around the corner. "Cooper? Naw don't think so." her head disappeared. She came back around carrying three cups of coffee. She had a puzzled look on her face as she placed the cups in front of Allan and Steven. She took a sip and said, "Oh my word, be forgetting my head next." She rose quickly and came back with a carton of milk and a sugar bowl. She had a furrowed brow and sat back down.

"Unless yer talking 'bout the Coopers over west road 84 by the Peterson farm? But that's way back. I was jus' a girl den." She took a sip of coffee. "I remember my folks talking about it. Hell, most ah da town were jawin' about it. Some bad bizness. A bear attack or sumptin." She looked at Allan.

"Ya, I 'member it too. I was a bit older than you, but it was my brothers that told me 'bout it. Sum said the little girl cut up her folks while they slept. Chopped dem up good and her brother and little sister. My brother said that they had heard that there was even blood on the ceiling. It was everywhere." He paused to take a sip of his coffee. His fingers stabbed the air.

"It weren't that little girl. My pa said she was just a little spit of a thing. No how could she have done the butchery that they said had bin done."

"Course dat was a long time back an can't be nuthin ta do with yer ma."

"Dat yer family name?" Doreen asked.

"Ya. My mother's family. She came from around here."

"Sorry, don't know any Coopers 'round here septin that old story."

"No, that's fine. Whatever happened to the girl?" Steven asked.

"Well, don't rightly know. Seems she disappeared. Jus' up and vanished from the cop shop still covered in blood an' all. Never heard 'bout her agin."

After coffee, Allan took Steven out to the back. Gunner walked alongside.

"You ever drove a tractor afore?" Allan asked.

"No, sir."

"Well, it ain't hard. I got a job fer ya. It ain't very exciting but needs doin'."

"Sure, anything I can do to help."

Allan climbed up and sat on the metal seat.

"C'mon up."

Steven mimicked Allan, grabbing the huge black tire and the top of the tractor. There was a step for his foot. Allan moved to give him room, then started the tractor. It started almost immediately with a roar, and a cloud of black smoke erupted from the exhaust pipe that stood straight up from the center of the tractor. He pointed at a series of three levers, chrome with black knobs. He pointed at the first one.

"Ya don't need ta worry 'bout this one. Just these two. This one is up, and this is down," he called over the engine's noise. He pushed one lever down and attached to the tractor a sort of a flat piece of iron moved down with a deep whine sound. Allan pulled on the next lever, and the flat iron moved up. Behind the piece of iron attached with chains to the tractor was a flat pallet of wood. There were a couple of rocks on the pallet.

"Got it?" He grinned as if he were imparting great difficult knowledge.

"Sure?" Steven said, not really sure. Allan grinned and shut the tractor off. It was suddenly really quiet.

"So like ah said, it ain't excitin' werk. Ya drive 'round this here field, and when ya see a stone, you drive over it and push down on the lever. That drops the picker down, and then you raise it and the rock lands on the float. That's it."

"That's it? Just pick up stones?" said Steven.

Allan started climbing down from the tractor. "Yup, that's it."

"Cool. Ok. I can do that."

"Ok, off you go. I'll flag ya down when it's suppertime."

Steven climbed in the seat of the tractor. The metal seat was surprisingly comfortable. Allan leaned forward. Steven pushed the red 'start' button, and the tractor came to life, spouting a black cloud. Allan nodded and smiled, hands on his hips.

"Oh, ya." He climbed up beside Steven.

"Ah forgot. That there." He pointed to a pedal next to Steven's left foot.

"That there is the clutch an' that there," he pointed to the pedal next to Steven's right foot, "is the brake, an' the throttle is here under the steering wheel." He grabbed a small lever sitting on a half-circle of metal. He pushed the lever to the right, and the engine sped up; the black smoke disappeared.

"You kin leave it there. Seecon gear is going to be fast enough." He looked at Steven skeptically. "You know haw ta drive stick?"

"Yes, sir," Steven said. Steven saw Allan sigh, relieved. He climbed down from the tractor and stepped back. Steven pushed down on the clutch, shifted into what he guessed was first and let the clutch out slowly. The tractor lurched forward, nearly throwing him backward off the seat. He pushed in the clutch.

Allan was grinning, with Gunner standing beside him. Steven moved the shifter into his second guess at first gear and let out the clutch. The tractor lurched forward and started to move. Steven grinned at Allan. Allan waved and started walking back to the barn, Gunner at his side.

It took a few tries to lower the picker enough to catch the stones, but not too far to grab a lot of dirt. But once he got it, he fell easily into a routine. The noise of the tractor faded. He found his mind wandered. He thought of his mom and her stories. So many stories, all of them quaint and otherworldly, like her, with her quiet elegance. Her soft-spoken ease. He got lost in the past, and it was a surprise when he heard a clanging. At first, he thought he had damaged the tractor; after a second, he looked around and saw Allan standing waving at him with Gunner not far off. Steven turned the tractor, lifted the rock picker, and drove to Allan. He shut the tractor off. Steven was shocked at the quiet. He stood. His ass was asleep. He climbed down slowly.

"Ya done good. Betcha, yer butt is on the sore side." Allan laughed.

Together they walked towards the house. It was near sunset. The trees cast long shadows across the yard. Everything had a warm feeling. Steven looked about, tired and content.

Gunner came loping from the trees to the north.

They got to the house. Steven noticed the large metal triangle hung by the back door. It had been the clanging he had heard. He smiled at the simplicity of it.

Inside, Doreen said, "Go wash up. Supper's ready."

Steven went into the small washroom. He was shocked at what he saw. His face was covered in grey-black dirt. His eyes nearly glowed out of his face. His lips stood out, pink and wet, and there were streaks running down the sides of his head from sweat. He washed. He had to work at getting the black from his nostrils, mouth and ears. He tasted the grit. He swished water around his mouth. It took a bit of time, but when he stepped out of the bathroom; he was more or less clean. He walked through the kitchen. It smelled wonderful.

"I thought we'd have a special meal for our guest," Doreen said.

Allan was already seated in his spot. He grinned as Steven walked in.

"Sure glad yer here. Mighta had grilled cheese sandwiches agin."

"I heard that, an' you ain't so hard done by."

"No, I ain't. Just funnin'. You know dat."

She grinned at him. He looked like a mischievous, old gnome.

"We're having roast chicken, fresh potatoes an' green beans from the garden. You come by at the perfect time. The garden is puttin' out like you never saw, an' I just butchered a few hens last week."

"Oh, boy." Allan leaned forward, childlike.

"That sounds wonderful. It smells amazing," Steven said.

As Doreen headed for the kitchen, she said, "Maybe after the dishes are cleared, you kin play us a tune on that there guitar ya got."

Steven stopped smiling. "I wish I could. I don't know how to play. It's not my guitar."

Allan looked up.

"It was my dad's."

"He was a player?" Allan asked.

"No. It's hard to explain."

Allan nodded as Doreen came in with a big roasting pan.

"Allan put down a towel." Allan reached behind him to the cupboard and pulled out a tea towel. He spread it out flat on the table to protect the surface. Doreen put the roasting pan on the cloth. She lifted the lid with a flourish. The roast chicken was browned to perfection, surrounded by potatoes. She smiled with pride and went back to the kitchen. She came back with steamed green beans and a gravy boat.

She sat with a sigh. She looked at the table, looked at Allan with love and to Steven with kindness. She reached for their hands and hung her head. Steven and Allan bowed to her.

She looked up, smiling.

"Well, let's eat."

She stood and took Steven's plate. She served him some potatoes.

"White or dark? Yer a dark meat kinda guy, aren't you.?" She smiled, and Steven nodded.

She piled his plate with chicken and beans and covered them with gravy. She handed Steven his plate.

"Enjoy."

"That's a lot of food." He smiled.

"Ya werked fer it."

She smiled as she served Allan.

"Thank you, dear," Allan said.

Still smiling, she served herself. She sat. Looked at her table and Allan and Steven. She ate. Again they ate in silence efficiently. When they were done, she cleared the dishes. She came back.

"I think the dishes kin wait this evening," she said, almost apologetically.

"How bout a round of Bunco, " she said.

Allan smiled and reached behind him to the cupboard. He pulled out a deck of cards.

Steven had never played Bunco, but he got a handle on it and hours passed. Doreen kept up a steady monologue about crops, old stories and town gossip.

Around 11, she just stopped. She looked up at Steven with sadness in her eyes.

"Is there anything we can say to you to stop you from heading to the crossroads? You seem happy here. Yer a good person and a good worker. Yer welcome to stay here. Our son has long since moved out. You can stay in his room. God knows we could use the help round here."

"Mother," Allan said quietly and touched her arm.

"I know.. I know." There were tears in her eyes."It's just such a waste." She looked at Steven. "That creature has ruined so many lives hereabouts." Angrily, she wiped the tears from her eyes.

She stood.

"It has been a real fine pleasure meeting you, Steven. I hope you find what you are searching for. Now it's time for a foolish old woman to find her bed. Goodbye, Steven." She squeezed his hand and left the room. They watched her go.

Allan looked at Steven, turned in his seat and pulled from the cupboard a mason jar with clear liquid and two shot glasses. He unscrewed the lid and filled the shot glasses. He put the lid on and put the jar back behind him in the cupboard. He pushed one of the glasses to Steven.

Steven hesitated, then reached out and took the glass.

Allan looked at the liquid.

"This here is the finest shine that'll ever touch to yer lips. A fella not far down the road brews it up. Name of Jacob."

"I met Jacob last night at Frank's."

"Ya, I'm not surprised. He's a stand-up guy." Allan paused.

"We should git going." Allan knocked the shot back.

Steven followed suit, bracing himself for the burn. A burn that didn't come. It was as smooth as any fine scotch in his father's liquor cabinet. He felt the warmth slide down his throat.

Allan looked at him, a smile playing on his lips. "Good stuff, Huh?"

"Yes," Steven said. "It's really good."

Allan chuckled.

"Let's go." He stood, and Steven followed as he left the house.

Outside it was dark. Off to the south was a strip of lighter blue, vibrant in the dark. The area in front of the garage was lit by a yardlight that cast deep shadows everywhere. Gunner came walking out from the shadows and climbed into the truck when Allan opened the door. Steven walked around the truck, put his backpack and guitar case in the back, and climbed in. The truck whined as they backed up and turned around.

Allan was quiet as they turned out onto 78, heading south. The cool night air came in the open windows. The sky was laced with stars. Steven felt calmer than he had in months. He was nearing his goal, and he felt no nervousness, just a sense of ease and well-being.

He looked out across the fields.

Allan cleared his throat. Steven could see he had something to say and was working up to it.

"Doreen is right. Nuthin good comes from meeting with The Judge an' I ain't getting any younger. You would be a great help." He paused. "What she didn't say.. Was...well, we had a son. He's gone. He's never coming back." Allan slowed the truck. Gunner watched him. He stopped and turned to look at Steven.

"He met with the Judge, and 6 years later he was gone. I never found out why..." Allan lapsed into silence. He pushed the truck into gear and started moving. "Just think about it. You can werk the farm and who knows one day it could be yers. It's a good farm. Bin good to me and mine." Allan didn't look at Steven.

"I'm not going to make a deal. I need to ask a question. That's it. I need to know why he killed my sister. That's it. I just need to know. And return his cursed guitar."

Allan didn't say anything. They drove in silence, staring ahead at the two yellowy puddles that led them down the road. Allan turned off the road and swung the truck around, stopping in the middle of the road.

"This is it." He checked the clock on the dash. It was almost midnight.

"Thank you for everything. I'm sorry about your son. I have to do this."

Allan looked straight ahead. He seemed not to hear. Steven got out of the truck and pulled his backpack and guitar from the back. He stood and looked at Allan. Allan looked at him.

"It was fine, meetin ya."

He completed his U-turn, and Steven watched as the weak taillights faded into the dark as the truck rattled away. It became quiet. Very quiet. Steven put his pack and guitar case down. The cool air carried the smell of earth, the sweet smell of growing crops, and water. A breeze stirred the grass along the side of the road.

Steven stood in the center of the crossroads. He looked down the road in each of the four directions. No lights could be seen on the road in any direction.

He jumped when, behind him, an engine revved loudly. He spun 'round and found a car stopped inches from his legs.

It was black and very shiny. Steven knew a bit about cars. Enough to recognize a '69 GTO. He chuckled to himself. Of course, the 69 GTO was often called The Goat. There was even a model called The Judge. It made sense.

The driver's door opened, and a man slid out. He was tall and dressed in a fine suit. He had a smile you could blind yourself looking at. Steven had seen that kind of smile before. His father had a smile like that, it never touched his eyes. This man's smile did not touch his eyes either. His eyes were dark and hard.

The Judge walked around his car, easy and supremely in his element.

"Howdy. Steven, isn't it?"

"Yes, my name is Steven. I brought you something."

"For me. How unusual. What is it?"

"It's the guitar you gave my father."

"Your father, really." He bent and opened the guitar case.

"My, my, this is one fine guitar." he pulled the guitar from the case. "This is a Kalamazooo KG-14 flat-top. You don't see those every day for sure." He held it with reverence. "But son, I never gave this to your dad."

He returned the guitar to its case, but left it open. He stood looking down at the guitar. When he looked up, Steven held a chrome long barrel .45 pointed at his head. The Judge smiled.

"You seem to be upset."

"Why'd you have to kill my sister?"

"Your sister? Son..."

"Stop calling me son I'm not your son." The gun was shaking in Steven's hand.

The Judge smiled.

"I never understand how anyone can think one of your weapons could possibly hurt me. I have been shot, stabbed, blown up and burned. I can't be hurt by...wait, what is..?"

The world exploded in light and noise. Steven turned to see what was happening and tripped, falling backwards. It saved his life. The semi-truck screamed past him, ramming into the Judge, then into the Judges' car. The noise was all-encompassing. The roar filled the world. The truck pushed what was left of the car and the Judge down the road and into the ditch.

Steven picked himself up from the road. It had been close, mere inches. He walked to the wreck.

The Judge stepped out of the ditch, brushing dirt from his lapel. He smiled at Steven.

They both looked up when the door to the ruined cab opened and a man stepped out. It was Gordon. He was bleeding heavily from a gash in his scalp. He fell from the cab onto the grass in the ditch.

"YOU!" Gordon screamed. "YOU! You can't have him." Gordon had managed to stand and was walking slowly toward Steven and the Judge. "You can't have him. Not till I get what you promised."

"But Gordon, that's not the deal."

"You didn't give me what I wanted. I never got what I asked for."

"Oh, Gordon, I think you did. You wanted to be free. You had some romantic notion about truck drivers. You wanted to drive a truck."

"Not forever!"

"Well, yes, however, you never specified for how long you wanted to be 'free' and really, it hasn't been forever. It's only been some 40 years." The Judge smiled. Gordon swayed, slumped to the blacktop. Steven ran to him.

"Hmmm. Looks like we are going to have a visit from Mr. White," the Judge said.

Gordon was sitting propped on one arm. He was bleeding badly. He looked at Steven, scowled, and looked at the Judge.

"You've got him. Now release me. I've driven for you long enough." Gordon said quietly.

"Now, Gordon. That's hardly fair. You got exactly what you asked for. You will continue to drive for me until I say otherwise. That's our deal."

"What did you say?" Steven asked Gordon. Gordon just looked at him, then back to the Judge. "What's he talking about?" Steven asked the Judge.

The Judge frowned. "Well, I sent him to pick you up, but instead, he just had to stop at Frank's. He just can't resist stopping at The Ol' Scratch. I tried to get Billy to drive you over, but Billy has become a bit difficult, listening to Jacob and his 'Jurors'." He made little air quotes with one hand. "So I got Allan to bring you here," the Judge said, finally.

Steven looked at the Judge, "Wait, Allan is marked?" he asked, confused.

"Oh Yeah. Both Allan and Doreen are."

"They were so against me coming here. Something to do with their son."

The Judge studied Steven for a minute; he said. "Yeah, they were upset about their son. His deal ran its course. They came to me, demanding I bring him back. So we made a deal."

"You brought their son back. You can do that?" Steven stepped forward.

"Well, yes, and no. I can plunk the soul back into their body. It's usually short and extremely painful, but their son had been cremated. No body, so I arranged for Gunner to have an accident and dropped their son into the dog's body. Of course, they're convinced I didn't hold up my end of the deal. Sad, really. Their son is right there." He paused and looked around. "Well shit," he said quietly. Steven followed his gaze.

At the side of the road the remains of the guitar and case lay, a pile of shattered splinters. The Judge walked over to where the pieces rested. He reached down and picked up the guitar, whole and undamaged. He held it before himself admiringly. He turned it back and forth.

"There is something about this guitar. I know this guitar. O'l Tom gave it to that fine young boy many years ago."

"Who's Ol' Tom?"

"Oh, no one." He glanced quickly at Steven, then back to the guitar. "Your dad must have had deep pockets."

He looked at Steven, holding the beautiful guitar.

"Now, Steven. About your situation. I'm sorry, but I never met your dad. If I had, I certainly would not have given him this guitar."

"LIAR!" Steven screamed, and raised the gun.

"Yes, I am a liar, however, not in this instance. I never met with your father, and I never made a deal with him." He smiled and straightened his already straight tie.

"I did meet with your mother, though."

The gun dropped with Steven's arm as it fell to his side.

"My mother?" he asked.

"Oh, yes. It was many years ago. She wanted to be free of her father. He wasn't a nice man. Quite abusive toward her and her little sister. Almost a monster, really. It was just shortly after I had arrived in this neck of the woods."

The Judge paused and looked at the guitar in his hand, then casually he tossed it. The ghost of the guitar vanished before it could hit the ground. The Judge looked down. Beside him on the pavement was the shattered guitar. Absently he said, "I can't fix this. It never entered my realm. Pity." He looked up at Steven. Behind the Judge, Steven noticed the 69 GTO stood whole and undamaged.

"Ah, I see Gordon has crossed over. I'll have to get him a new rig." The Judge smiled.

Steven looked to where Gordon lay. He wasn't breathing.

"Yes, I gave your mother what she wanted. She was quite a woman. She wanted two things. I usually don't go for that sort of contract, but like I said, I was new to the area. We came to an agreement." He smiled. Not his big shit-eating grin, but a smaller, almost sheepish grin.

"I may have been a bit too enthusiastic with my efforts to help her."

"The bear attack?"

"Bear? Yes, well, it wasn't a bear. I released a hellhound. They can be messy," he looked out across the dark fields.

"Then I pushed your mom forward in time a bit until the excitement died down around her, and I gave her the second part of her contract."

Steven took a step backward.

"Ah, you have a sense of it. Yes, Steven. I gave her, you. She wanted a son, so I gave her my own."

"No," Steven said. "No."

"Haven't you noticed you are a bit different? How people seem to get hurt around you? It's in your nature."

"No."

"You are my son, Steven, and I have such great hopes for you."

Steven looked at this man in front of him and knew it was true. People had always gotten hurt around him. The more he loved them, the more they got hurt. He cried then. He had loved his little sister so much.

"NO!" He screamed and brought the gun he still held in his hand up to his chin and pulled the trigger.

The report was massive. The sound exploded out. A physical wave carried past the Judge into the night.

Steven never heard the crack of the .45 round. Never heard it echo over the fields. The round tore through Steven's face and head, ripping it to shreds, scattering blood, bone, and brain into the night air. It snapped what was left of his head backward. It tossed his body up and back. Steven's body landed several feet away on the pavement with a wet crunch.

The Judge picked up the gun and walked over to where what was left of Steven lay. He looked down at him for a time. He looked up at the sky with its millions of stars. Off to the west, he noticed the yard light of a farm. To the east, just over the horizon, he could see the soft glow of the far-off city. He looked back to Steven as he lay on the hard blacktop.

"The young are so impulsive. You have to love their passion and spontaneity." He looked at the heavy chrome gun in his hand.

"You will find that you are very hard to kill."

Steven's face began to reform itself. His ripped flesh knitting itself. Jawbone growing, stretching to meet the front part of his skull. Muscle and skin stretched across the newly formed bone. It only took a minute. Steven shifted, coughed, and new eyelids opened. He looked confused, laying on his back, his eyes darted around. He sat bolt upright.

"Wait! What the fuck is going on?"

The Judge walked closer to Steven and extended his hand.

"I told you, you are my son." He helped Steven to his feet. "And I have so many plans for us." He slid his arm around Steven. "Come on, let's go. Hey, you want to drive?"

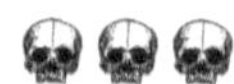

A COLD HAND

THE STRANGE DISAPPEARANCE OF
JOHN WHITEY BURNETT

4

THE STRANGE DISAPPEARANCE OF JOHN WHITEY BURNETT

Prologue

On a cool night in August, an unassuming man walked into O'l Tom's Backroom to take part in an open mic. This wasn't unusual. Open mics happened all around the city. It was a staple of the music venues to open the stage once a week to the amateurs, the wannabes and the up and comers with a guitar and a song to sing. John 'Whitey' Burnett was no different. He had a song and a dream. What made this night different was what transpired that evening and the subsequent fallout in the audience.

John Whitey Burnett was the fictional persona adopted by Dwain Marsh. By all accounts, he was not a very good player. Some even describe him as torturous to listen to. He was somewhat known in the indie music scene for his disastrous renditions of the only two songs he ever played and his dream that he told everyone he spoke to. His greatest dream was to "wake the devil and make him cry." After years of being part of the open mic scene, he disappeared. Some say for several months, others say for a couple of years. No one knows where he went or what he had been doing. There are a few reports that he spent time in the delta and found a voodoo queen that gave him magical ability with the guitar. This, of course, is just stories, but they all agree the night he reappeared was a night that destroyed the lives of nearly all that were there.

Now, all these years later, very few people know who John 'Whitey' Burnett was. The few that do mostly wish they did not. Knowing him means they know what happened to him. That knowledge haunts them and will for the rest of their lives.

Many of the audience could not be located, and of those we found, most refused to talk about what happened to them that night and the days, months, and years afterwards. What follows is the testimony of eight of the individuals who have agreed to relive that night, some reluctantly.

Recently, several notebooks surfaced on eBay claiming to be John 'Whitey' Burnett's. How they were obtained seems to be suspect. When questioned, the seller of these books was vague about how he came by them and refused to be interviewed; however, he agreed to have them authenticated. It took several months of research. John/Dwaine did indeed own these books, and it is certain that the contents are his.

Published here for the very first time are some sketches produced by John 'Whitey' Burnett (Dwain Marsh) leading up to that evening.

Chapter 1
Ryan the host

We sat by the window of Ol' Tom's backroom early on Saturday afternoon in July. Ryan has agreed to tell his take on what took place many years ago while he was hosting his Wednesday night open mic.

"Dwain came in that night, oh ya sorry, John came in that night, and I could tell something was different. First of all, it was busy. It was never that busy on a regular open mic. Wednesdays were usually pretty slow. But the place was full, and the playlist was nearly full as well. John walked up to put his name down. I hadn't seen him for some time. But he looked different. I don't know how to describe it. He was thinner and looked haggard. Maybe he had been sick. There was an intensity to him that I hadn't seen in him before. And he wasn't carrying that fucking guitar he usually played."

"He had a bad guitar?"

"Ya, it's terrible. Not the one he played that night. He usually played a cheap thing he bought online. Then he made it even worse by painting it black with fucking voodoo signs and symbols. The poor guitar probably didn't have good tone, to begin with, but the paint just killed it, and they didn't mean shit, but he thought the symbols gave it an air of mystery as if he was from the south. Bullshit. He's just a white boy from around here. He wouldn't know the blues if it bit him on the ass."

"I gather you didn't like John."

"Nah, he was OK. He had some strange ideas, and he couldn't play for shit, at least before. Like I said, that night was different. He had a different guitar. It looked old or well, it looked OK when he first brought it in."

"You mean it changed?"

"Well, ya. It became new as he played it."

"I don't understand."

"No, neither do I. It got newer as he played. I can't describe it any other way. It got newer. It was a strange night."

He sits back and looks out the window at the rain, lost in the memories.

"And you hadn't seen this guitar before?"

He returned from wherever he had gone.

"No. It wasn't his usual guitar like I said."

"And he always plays the same two songs. You'd think he'd get better at playing them, but he didn't. Tonight was different. He started with a song I had never heard before. It was good. Really good. I was watching his hands. There were chord progressions I had never heard before. It was unique. And oh ya, his fingers were bleeding."

"Bleeding?"

"Yes. He was in pain, but it didn't stop him from playing. It was brilliant. I had never seen him play that well. I mean, not ever. The next song was angry, almost violent. I remember thinking how it must hurt like hell to play that hard with his torn-up fingers."

"Do you remember any of the lyrics?"

"No, that's the other weird thing. I can't. I've tried. I've tried reproducing the chord changes, and I just can't get them. I can't remember them at all."

"Do you remember how many songs he played that night?"

After a pause.

"I think twelve, no, thirteen. But I'm not a hundred percent sure. My memory gets fuzzy when I try to focus on the night. And it's been years."

"Is it usual that you let someone play more than two songs?"

"No, not usual. Normally it's fairly strict. A two song limit. It kept things fair. Also, if someone was shitty, you only had to listen to two songs, then they were gone."

"Why did you let John play more than two songs?"

"I really don't know. I do remember that fucking guitar getting shiny as John played. Then everything changed. He started playing a song different from the others. I couldn't tell you what made it different. It was a different voice. It was terribly honest. It tore at me. It was as if he had reached inside me and sang my deepest fears and regrets. I felt embarrassed."

I noticed John was crying as he played, but the weird thing was when his tears fell on the strings, they sizzled as if the strings were hot. I couldn't understand how that could be. I checked the board, and it was dark. I panicked. I started checking cables. Then I noticed a burnt insulation smell.

The next day I checked the board. It was completely fried. The inside was black. Never saw anything like it. Not before, not since. It was completely gutted."

"Did you notice anything else out of place?"

"Ya, there was a dog with really weird eyes. One looked like it was completely white, but not like huskies. It was just blank."

"Was the dog blind?"

"No, no, nothing like that. It was… it was fucking freaky, is what it was. I like dogs. This dog gave me the creeps.

Actually, it scared me. I was watching it when they first walked in, thinking Judy was going to be pissed that someone brought a dog into his bar. When that dog looked at me, I had to look away."

"Anything else?"

"Ya… Ya… When John left the stage, he just dropped his guitar. It shattered like it was made of glass. There was almost nothing left. I swept up later. Wait, no, I didn't. That's odd. I left. I went home and fell asleep. I swept up the next day. I forgot about that. I can't believe Judy let me leave the stage in such a mess. But he didn't seem to be put out about any of it. He was even cool about the fried board. He just bought a new one. Had it the next day ready to go. Honestly, it was weird. He usually is a bastard about anything that cost him money. You know, he was off the entire night, now I think about it. Acted way too cheerful. Like it was a special night. It wasn't just another open mic. I guess that's not right, though, cause it turned out to be a special night if you can call it 'special'."

Chapter 2
Anonymous Was In The Audience.

We are sitting in an elegant glass solarium in a fine house in an upscale neighbourhood. It's just after lunch on a Tuesday in August. The solarium overlooks a well-manicured garden with a fountain. J, she has asked not to be identified, returns with coffee and sits across from me. She's a handsome woman in her sixties. She smooths her skirt and glances around. She's obviously nervous. The house is quiet like it's holding its breath. Once it had been filled with her teenagers now, she only waits for her husband.

"You won't publish my name?"

"No, as we agreed, you will remain anonymous."

"You were at Ol' Tom's back room that night?"

"Yes. Yes, I was. I just went to listen to the music."

"Were you there to play?"

"Yes."

"Did you go often?"

"A long pause."

"Yes... I think I should explain something. My marriage at that time was not in a good space. My husband was working long hours and was rarely home. We had three young children. I had always wanted to sing on stage. You know I was in a band in high school."

She looks down at her hands.

"I only want to know what you witnessed that night. You can tell me as much or as little as you want."

She straightens her skirt again and glances at the door.

"I was signed up to play. I had written a new song with my music partner."

"Did you know John?"

"No, before that night, I had never seen him. I was seated a couple of tables back from the stage. He walked past. I thought he looked like a bum. Sorry I mean a street person.

He looked rough. He was carrying a dark guitar. His hands were all torn up. They had dried blood on them."

She glanced once more at the front door.

"What happened next?"

"I...he went to the host and signed his name on the sheet. The host seemed to know him. They didn't talk. I don't think. But he recognized John, I'm sure of it.

John walked to an empty table near the back of the room and sat just holding his guitar and staring straight ahead."

"Did he talk to anyone?"

"No, not even the server. She went up to him, but he ignored her."

"It was dark there, the only light coming from the stage, and his eyes seemed to glow."

"John's?"

"Yes. They had an intensity. It's hard to describe. He was so focused."

"The host started the evening by playing a couple of tunes. I forget what he played, but I had heard them before. He's good. After he sat by the soundboard and called the first name on the list."

"What was John doing?"

"Honestly, I don't know. I was watching the stage."

She shifts in her seat.

"When did you notice him again?"

"When his name was announced. I remember I was surprised because he had signed up late so would have been called much later in the evening."

"Did you notice anything else?"

"Well, yes, but… I'm not sure if I noticed then or afterwards."

"What do you mean?"

"Well, a man was standing at the back of the room. I didn't see him arrive. He was watching John walk to the stage. The weird thing was he had a dog with him. I don't think dogs were allowed in the cafe. But there he was. He was very handsome, dressed in a suit.

It seemed like the host called John the moment he saw the man standing there."

"Did John see the man?"

"I don't know. I don't think so. He walked to the stage and started to play without waiting for the host to announce him. Just started right in. Didn't even say what the song was called.

I don't remember much of the song. It was nice; I think. John was very intense. I think he played a couple of songs, but I can't remember."

"What happened then?"

"After he played,? There seemed to be a problem with his guitar. I think he broke a string. I don't really remember. I guess I drank more than I thought. Anyway, John seemed to smile, then dropped his guitar on the ground and walked off the stage. I never saw him leave."

"Did you see the man with the dog leave?"

"Dog? Oh ya, no, I don't know what happened to him. Never saw him again."

"What happened next?"

"Nothing. It was late, and I went home?"

Chapter 3
David Was Tending Bar

I met David at a busy bar in the Annex. He's tending bar. I get the feeling he is annoyed by my questions.

"I don't know, man. It was one of those nights, ya know. Just a weird night."

"You were bartending at Ol' Tom's?"

"Ya, ya. Had been for almost a month. Weird bar ran by this chick named Judy. He was an OK guy. I liked working there. Sometimes, the music was pretty good. Not always though. Sometimes it was shit."

"Do you play?"

"Fuck no! But I know what I like." He leaves to pull several pints for the server. "Like I said. It was just a weird night."

"How was it weird?"

"Well, for starters, it was Wednesday. They're always a bit weird, but this Wednesday night was even weirder. It was packed. The open mic night was never packed. But that night, there wasn't an empty table. Very weird. Judy was happy, so was the server. I don't remember her name. A cute blonde." He chuckles, then looks at me. "I don't know. There was something in the air."

"Did you know John?"

"Naw. I'd seen him a couple times. He wasn't very good." He pauses and wipes the counter. "Actually, he was terrible. I don't think he could even tune that shitty guitar he had."

"Did you see him arrive that night?"

"No, I think I was out back having a smoke when he came in. The server came to place the orders complaining that Dwain was ignoring her. I mean he wasn't a big tipper or anything, but he always was friendly and was good for a couple of beers but this night nothing."

"Dwain?"

"Dwain ya, that's his real name. Not John Whitey Burnett. He just made that shit up to sound cool. He was one of the most uncool dudes I ever saw. I mean that man was just a square. I did see the other man come in with the dog. Dogs aren't allowed in the bar. It was against the law, but Judy just nodded as the man walked in. Never said a word. That dog scared me. I'm not gonna lie."

"Did Judy know the man?"

"Ya, I think so. To be honest, Judy seemed scared of the man. I asked him about the man. Judy lost it. Nearly got my face chewed off. I thought I was going to get fired. But Judy calmed down and told me to mind my own business."

"What happened next?"

"The music started. It was pretty good that night. I got into a groove and the night was going good. Then I heard John start his first song. I can't remember what it was, but it was good I think. Then he was done. I heard gasps from the crowd. I looked up. From the bar I couldn't really see the stage, really. I saw a flash of light and then John walked past me. No guitar, just walked out followed by the dude in the suit and his fucking dog."

"Then?"

"Then nothing. The bar emptied pretty quick. Again, it was a weird night. It had just turned 12 that's very early for musicians to pack it in but by one we were counting out the tips. Judy seemed relieved."

"Anything else."

He looks down at his feet, leaning forward on the bar. "Ya. Ya, a couple of things. When John left, I wiped my face, and it was wet like I had been bawling."

"Had you been?"

"Don't think so."

"And the other thing?"

"I haven't had an easy night since then. Every night since then i have had these fucking dreams that scare the shit out of me. I mean, these dreams are fucking awful. I have to take sleeping pills just to get some sleep.

Chapter 4
Bradley, A Songwriter

We are sitting on a park bench in the afternoon, not far from Ol' Tom's. Bradley is shaking. He obviously has had a few bad years and has been living rough for some time. He had only agreed to this interview after I promised to pay him twenty dollars.

"You were at Ol' Tom's that night?"

He twitches and looks at me with hollow eyes. "Ya fuck, I was there."

"Can you tell me what you saw?"

"Ya, well I guess so. I was there. OK I don't like to talk about it. It was the worst night of my life, OK? I fucking hate that place."

"O'l Tom's?"

"Ya, fucking Ol' Tom's. That's where it all turned to shit."

"What do you mean?"

He looks at me. I can see pain in his eyes. "I had been going to Ol' Tom's for a couple of months before that night. I was writing a lot then and was recording a new album. I used the open mic to try out new songs. Get an idea of how the audience liked the songs. Worked pretty good. Then fucking John Whitey Barnett happened. He walked in and tore everything from me."

"I don't understand."

"After that night I couldn't write. I couldn't play. It was all gone. Just gone. I don't remember what he played. I remember thinking that he was good, powerful. His songs reminded me of Robert Johnson's music, but I can't remember any of it now. I do remember the feeling something was sucking out my soul."

"Maybe start at the beginning."

"Ya, ya sure. OK, I got there maybe ten-thirty or so. I spent the day in the studio. I was feeling frustrated. It hadn't been going well. It was missing something. It just wasn't coming together. My engineer was happy. He thought it was great. I hated it all. I had planned to drink some beer and maybe find a spark in the raw music on stage."

"Did you?"

"No. I sat down near the front with a friend of mine. I remember being surprised how full the place was. Usually, the open mic was kinda sparse, but the bar was packed.

John was already sitting at a table near the back. I had hoped I had missed his set. He was pretty bad. I don't think John Whitey Burnett is his real name. It sounds fake.

The air in the room shifted. I looked around to see what had happened. It was like lights flickered or someone famous walked in. Ya, know Bob Dylan played there once." He smiles at the legend. "Anyway, it wasn't anyone famous, but there was this guy leaning against the back wall. He looked; I don't know. He looked powerful. He was dressed in a suit, but there was something about him. He was smiling. He was slick like maybe he was a music executive or something.

And oh ya, he had a strange dog with him. Never seen a dog in there before. Anyway, I just noticed the man when the host called John to the stage."

"Can you describe what happened?"

"Not really. It's all very foggy, and it's been years. I don't even remember how many songs he played, but I remember the last one. Not the words or even the melody, but I remember how it made me feel. It was the song I always wanted to write. It was a song that was in me waiting to be written. It was my song. My last song."

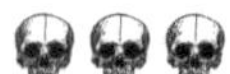

Chapter 5
Spike, A Bass Player

Spike, not his real name, sits beside me at the bar. He has just come off stage. He pushes his long hair back from his face and grins at me.

"So, you want to know about Whitey?"

"Yes, specifically the night he vanished."

"That was a spectacularly fucked up night." He shakes his head and takes a deep swallow of the draft the bartender placed in front of him. "I'd known Whitey for a couple years before he vanished. We had started talking about doing a record. He had some pretty good songs written but I don't know, he just gave up. Stopped coming to the open stages. Even pawned his guitar. It wasn't a great guitar. Just a cheap Epiphone he had painted."

"Were you at Ol' Tom's that night?"

"I sure as shit was. I was sitting one table over from him. Saw him come in. Knew right off, things were different. He didn't say hi or nothing. Just walked past. I couldn't figure how he got his old guitar back but then I saw it was something else. Looked like a Kalamazoo, but it couldn't have been. This one was pretty badly beat up."

"A Kalamazoo?"

"Ya, it's one of the guitars Robert Johnson played. You know who Robert Johnson is, right?"

"Yes, I know about Robert Johnson."

"Whew. You had me worried there for a minute."

"Why is that?"

"If you don't know about Robert Johnson, you wouldn't be able to understand Whitey and what happened to him." He takes another swallow of his pint. "Anyway, Whitey walked past me up to the host and signed his name, then walked back and sat at a table. I watched him, trying to catch his eye. He didn't see me, or at least he didn't respond. It was very weird. I didn't think about him much after that for a while. I watched the next couple of acts then it all changed."

"Changed? How?"

"The air thickened. I mean it thickened. It felt like people slowed down. It was like everything was in slow motion. I looked around to see if other people noticed, or if it was just me. Other people had noticed. Many people were looking around. I turned to look at Whitey. He sat still, just staring at the stage. That's when I saw him."

"Him?"

"Ya. The man leaning against the back wall. He was very handsome, dressed in a dark suit. He had on one of those cowboy ties. What are they called? String tie, no Bolo tie. That's it. He had on a bolo tie with a silver skull and there was a dog. I mean a real live dog sitting beside him."

"A DOG! Fuck, it was so weird. A dog."

"Anyway, then the host called Whitey's name. I turned and watched Whitey stand and walk up to the stage. It was weird. It wasn't his turn. I'm sure of it. He had come in late, and they call your name based on the list, but there he was on stage. He sat on the chair and without uttering a word, started. Fuck, what a song. It tore my heart out. It was that good and that terrible. I was crying like a baby."

"I don't remember what he sang after that. I just know I felt horrible. Each song made me feel worse. I don't know; it was awful then he sang another song, and I cried again but this time I felt hope. I felt like it was going to be OK."

"Do you remember how many songs he sang?"

"No, I don't remember. Eight, maybe ten? Don't remember. It's all kinda fuzzy. I know he played several songs, each more horrific than the last except the last one, but I don't really remember.

Actually, since that night whenever I think about it. Whenever I try to remember what had happened. I get this headache. I mean a real head splitter."

"Everytime?"

"Yes, every time. It's terrible. I want to remember. I want to remember those fucking songs. They were powerful and I want to play them."

"Play them?"

"Yes. They… I know they would change my life. Songs that powerful could make me famous."

"Is that what you want? To be famous?"

He looks at me with a puzzled look. "Doesn't everyone? Absolutely I want to be famous." He finished his pint and ordered another.

"What happened after Whitey played his last song?"

Spike comes back from wherever his mind had gone and looks at me.

"He stared at the audience for a long time. I watched him sitting there, holding his guitar. The audience seemed stunned. They sat still, blank eyed and kind of vacant. He just sat there, then he stood, dropped his guitar and walked out of the bar. I watched him leave. I guess I was in shock or something. I just sat there. I didn't move. Just watched him go."

"Did you see what happened to the handsome man and the dog?"

"No, I never saw him leave. I never saw either of them again. I have searched but these headaches stop me."

Chapter 6
Abbey Was The Server

She meets me in the park a couple of blocks from O'l Tom's.

"Hi, Abbey. Thanks for meeting with me."

"Sure, no problem."

"What can you tell me about that night?"

"Worst fucking night of my life. I have had trouble working ever since and I haven't worked a restaurant since. That night changed everything for me."

"Can you tell me what happened?"

"Sure. I remembered being excited. The night started out great. We had a completely full house. I was making tips like crazy. I was running 'round busy as hell, but it was good. I was thinking I could take a couple of days off. Then Dwain walked in."

"You mean John, John whitey Burnett."

"Ha, ya, John Whitey Burnett. Fuck. you know that wasn't his real name?"

"Yes, I do."

"Well, John (she makes air quotes) came in, signed up and sat near the back at an empty table. I was surprised he found a table, but it was like the table was waiting for him or something. People seemed to not see it or ignored it. I don't know. Anyway, he sat, and I went to get his order. He usually orders a beer, maybe two, but that night he completely ignored me. It was as if I wasn't there. It was weird. But like I said, it was mad busy and I didn't have time to worry about it."

"When did you notice John next?"

"John? What I noticed next was the dude that walked in with a big fucking dog. I looked at Dave, he was working the bar. He just shrugged. I looked around and found Judy, the owner, and he just nodded 'it's OK' and waved me off. Judy seemed thrilled. At the time I thought it was because it was so busy but I think it was because of something else."

"Something else?"

"Ya, I think Judy knew the dude with the dog."

"Knew him? Why do you think that?"

"It was the way Judy hovered around the man. I never saw them talk but Judy seemed to be very excited or nervous to see him, like he was Judy's boss or something."

"His boss?"

"Ya, it was weird. The man never even looked at Judy, but I think Judy was a bit afraid of him. And that fucking dog. Every time I looked over, it was looking at me. It was terrifying."

"What happened when John stepped up to the stage?"

"I wasn't in the room at the time. I had slipped out to grab a smoke. When I came in, it was shocking. Everything had changed. Everyone was silent, just watching John on stage. I had never seen the room so quiet and many of them were crying. I couldn't believe it. I'm not sure how many songs John had played at the time, but I had never seen so many people sobbing. It was like a funeral or something.

I noticed the dude with the dog was smiling. There was a glitter in his eyes. He was really enjoying the music or maybe the response.

Judy was around the corner, watching the dude. He had an odd look on his face, kind of a nervous happiness or excitement. I'm not sure. I never saw Judy like that before."

"Have you seen him react that way since?"

"Ha, no I quit the next day. I have never walked into that place since and I have never seen Judy again."

"What happened after you saw Judy?"

"Judy saw me and positively beamed. It was unnerving. Actually, it was horrific. There was a ghoulishness to him. Really repulsive."

"I looked away and then I heard the music. It was terrible stuff. I never heard anything like it. It made my heart hurt."

"Your heart hurt?"

"Yes, it positively made my heart hurt. It was like all the hate in the world was poured into it. I felt crushed by it. I nearly fainted from what I heard. I had to lean against the wall to stop myself from falling over. I saw John on stage through a black tunnel. He was playing, his head down. When I looked away, I saw the dude against the wall with the dog, grinning an evil grin." She pauses. "I don't know if I should tell you this or if you will believe me but I swear I saw something else when I looked at him."

"What did you see?"

"I saw a horrible face. Not a man's but something else, something so terrible I have trouble even describing it. It was that face that made me quit work. I still see that face at night when I am trying to sleep. It's why I have had such a hard time since that night. The face I saw was pure evil. It was the Devil." She is crying as she says this. She wipes the tears away. "I never want to see that face again."

Chapter 7
Pria Was There By Accident

David the bartender that night called me a week or so after we had spoken and said he remembered a woman who had come into the bar just before JWB started to play. He said he remembered her because she was in a foul temper, cursing, ordered a double scotch straight up and knocked it back in one swallow. Then she ordered another. He had chuckled at the memory.

He gave me all the info he could remember. I wasn't sure I could find someone with just a first name, but I reached out to my detective friend, and he found her. I did not ask how.

She had moved from the city but agreed to a phone interview.

"Hi Pria. Thank you for agreeing to the interview."

"I'm not sure how much use I can be. I never went there before or since. I just went in to use the phone. It was a deeply shitty night.

"I'm sorry. Could you tell me what happened?"

"My car got towed. I only stopped to use the phone."

"The bartender said you had a drink."

She chuckled. "Ya, like I said. I wasn't having a good night."

"Because your car was towed?"

"No, well yes that was part of it. I just needed a drink." There's a long pause on the line. "Alright. I had a major blow out with my girlfriend. It was the worst. In fact, we broke up that night. I spent hours screaming then I went down, and my car was gone.

"I'm sorry."

"Ya me too. I'm not sure I could tell you. I got there and yes, I had a drink. Actually I had a couple then this guy walked in. I shivered like I got a chill, like I had a fever or something. It ran up my spine and my hand shook so bad I spilled my drink."

"Had you seen him before?"

"The guy that walked in? No, hell no. I couldn't recognize him now. If he walked in now, I wouldn't know him. When he walked past me, I nearly passed out. I stopped breathing.

You know when the edges of your sight narrows and gets black. That's what it was like. My heart was racing. I must have looked bad cause as soon as the guy walked past, the bartender touched my hand and asked me if I was OK. I flinched when he touched my hand. I broke into a sweat. I remember I got instantly angry then this fucking dog walks up to me, sits and just looks at me with these fucking eyes, ya know."

"Was the dog with the man who walked in?"

"How the fuck would I know. Look, I got to go."

"Just two more questions."

Heavy sigh and a long pause. "K. Fine. What?"

"Did you hear any of the music that night?"

"Music? Ya it started after a few minutes. I think. I'm not sure. The fucking dog stared at me for a minute then sniffed me. I swear it seemed like it winked at me before it walked into the back room." There's another long pause. "That dog really bothered me. Not just because it was a freaky looking dog but because he seemed to know me, like it really knew me, knew who I was right to the core. I felt so exposed I was embarrassed." Another long pause, "Look, I'm not feeling very well. That night made me question everything. I wasn't the cheeriest person for sure but after that I had to have serious therapy and I still don't sleep well. Some nights are OK others well fuck, I end up curled in the dark crying till the sun comes up. You know what, I can't. I just can't."

The phone went dead.

Chapter 8
Maria Was In The Audience

The young woman that sits across from me is beautiful and very young. She has agreed to speak with me after several calls. She is very reluctant.

"Thank you for agreeing to speak with me. Can you tell me about that night?"

"I'm not happy remembering that night. I have endured a lot of therapy surrounding that fucking night. I don't want to be here, but you are very persistent. Yes, I was there. My mom was playing, or at least she was going to play. She took me to a lot of these open mics. It was fun. I liked the music most of the time and I loved seeing her on stage. She was so happy singing her songs, but they often went late, and she would find a corner for me to sleep until it was time to go home."

"Is that what happened that night?"

"Yes, I had watched a few of the acts, but it was a busy night, and we hadn't got there early enough for her to get on the list, but she wanted to stay for the music. She was excited. She said the room felt different.

Beside the stage where the guitar players left the guitar cases was a bench. Mom took me there to sleep. She was seated at a table almost right beside where I would be sleeping.

I went to sleep. When I woke up, the room really had changed. At first, I couldn't make out what was happening. The audience was frozen, like they were hypnotised or something. They stared straight at the stage, unblinking. They

were crying. I looked at my mom. She was the same. I called
her but she couldn't hear me."

"That's when I saw the devil."

"The devil?"

"Yes. I saw him. I was the only one not looking at the
stage and leaning against the back wall was a tall man in a suit
and he was smiling. He looked like a man, but he wasn't. I
watched him. He was surrounded by cobwebs, dark thin lines
that stretched out in every direction, touching each person in
the audience, tugging at their minds, their hearts. And with
each note, the threads thickened. They wrapped around each
person in loops of dark. The song ended and the man's smile
was a terrible thing. He was on the brink of laughing when
another song began. This song was different. It touched the
air with hope. And love. The dark webs blew apart like smoke,
crumbled into wisps that floated away, and the man's smile
froze. His smile withered. The tendrils of black swirled around
him and his dog, then they were gone."

"What happened next?"

"The audience seemed to wake. Slowly regaining their
senses. I saw my mom look around, confused, then she
saw me. The man on stage stood. Everyone looked at him.
He dropped his guitar and walked out of the bar. My mom
came to me and asked if I was OK. We left the bar, and mom
stopped going to those open mics. She was never the same
again. Something died in her that night. And three years later,
she did die.

I have never forgotten the man and his dark web. I know
what I saw. The Devil is real."

I had hoped to find some conclusion, to find a definitive answer to what happened that night and maybe a clue to what ultimately happened to JWB. After meeting these people and hearing their stories, I cannot honestly say that I know what happened. I know the facts. I know Dwain styled himself a blues player. He named himself John Whitey Burnett. He was obsessed with the Robert Johnson story. Somehow, he became convinced that if he could 'wake' the Devil, he could make a deal and become a blues legend. He spoke of his dreams to anyone who would listen.

There is no conclusive proof he succeeded. It would be impossible to prove that the Devil showed up to listen to JWB. So we are left with more questions than answers. Speculation that his obsession led to some sort of psychic break that created a form of mass hypnosis. Other theories include there was a form of LSD in the beer taps that night produced from unclean hoses or added to the beer itself as a joke or elaborate hoax.

After meeting these people and hearing their stories, I cannot honestly say that I know what happened. I know the facts, but even they are suspect.

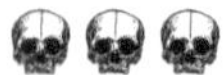

A COLD HAND

125

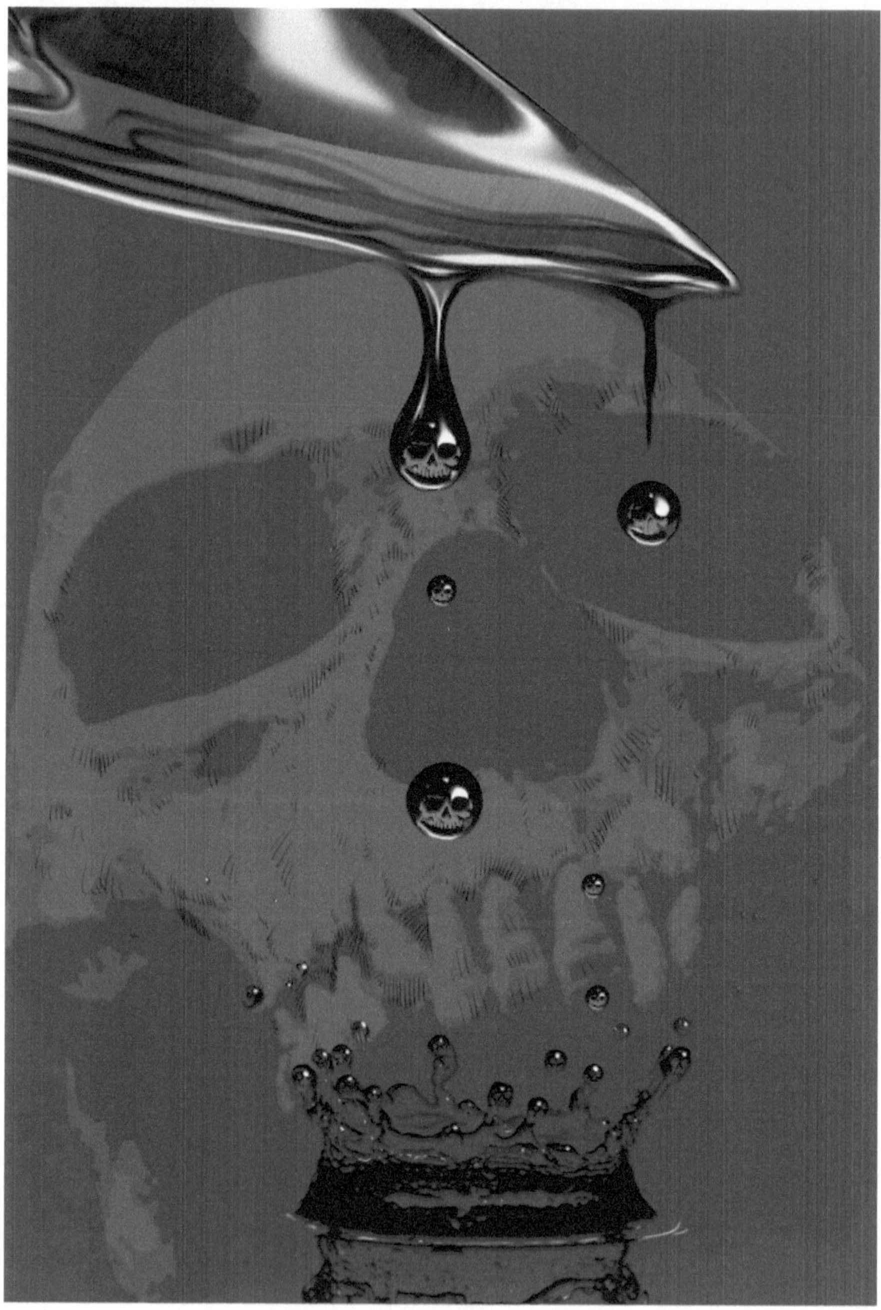

5

REPEATER

The man had been walking since before sunrise the day before. His eyes were fixed on the cracked pavement a few feet in front of him. They were set deep in dark circles and held a manic glow. His hands were stained dark, as if dipped in deep red paint nearly to the elbow, moved easily by his side, a steady rhythm, almost robotic. He walked along the cracked edge of the tarmac beside the grassy ditches, past the cans, beer bottles, litter and the occasional roadkill that was strewn along his path. He was dressed in jeans and a t-shirt, heavy boots, the laces dragged with each step all darkly stained. The black strip of pavement stretched out in front of him cutting a straight line through the fields of shades of green, gold, and bright yellow dotted with small islands of clumped trees that often concealed, old machinery or abandoned farmyards or just a large immovable rock. The sun rose over him. It thundered down on him as if attempting to flatten him to the ground, to pin him to the pavement and stop him. Stop his progress.

He was not hitchhiking. The man walked with purpose. He had a place to be, and he was determined to get there. When a car or truck passed, he never looked up.

Stanley Robertson passed him twice, waving both times just to be neighbourly. Both times, the man ignored him. He passed on the way over to Jacob's grabbing some of his fine shine and the second time when he came back disappointed and empty-handed.

The sun beat down on him. It was a hot day, clear and bright, with a cloudless sky. It was early afternoon when he walked past the O'l Scratch Tavern on the opposite side of the highway. No one noticed or, if they did, they did not comment.

He did not pause or even glance at the flashing lights and noise of the O'l Scratch. He did not seem to even notice. He walked on, each step one after another shuffling step. He never slowed, he never hurried, merely kept his steady pace completely focused on the road just ahead of his next step.

An hour later, he came to the junction of eleven and seventy-eight. His pace never slowed. He turned, heading south on seventy-eight.

It was late in the afternoon when he reached his goal. Sweat stuck his hair to his forehead and made dark stains on his t-shirt. The sun was still high enough to have some strength. The man stood at the side of the road beside a stop sign and did not notice the sweat as it rolled down his forehead and down his spine.

His focus did not waver. He became part of the landscape. The small animals slowly returned to their foraging. Insects buzzed and clicked around him. A car drove by the driver did not notice him standing there. The cloud of dust that trailed the car passed the man in a rush. He squinted his eyes slightly against it.

Dark crept upon him as the sky shifted, passing through a kaleidoscope of ever deeper shades of blue. The horizon's edge was a bright yellow, then peach, then pink, and finally a vibrant blue. As the colours left the world, the night sounds filled the surrounding fields. Mosquitoes harassed him. He did not seem to notice. He did not wave at them. Far off an owl called to the night announcing it's time to hunt. A dog replied, its bark echoed in the distance and still the man stood still, waiting.

The stains on his clothing had dried darker. On his hands, the dark stain shrivelled and cracked, enhancing his wrinkles and crevasses before it flaked off, dropping to the cooling pavement.

The moonless night wore on. Far off, a yard light marked a farmyard. The dog barked again. He waited.

When the lights of a car flared right beside him, he did not flinch. This is what he had been waiting for.

The slick man that stepped out of the car frowned. An unusual expression for this man, replaced by his customary chrome plated shark smile he wore most often.

"Why James, so nice to see you again. I am sorry to be late. I had no appointments this fine evening." He looked up at the dark sky. "I didn't think I would see you for… well, a while."

"I didn't get what you promised. It wasn't like it's supposed to be."

"But James, I don't promise how you'll feel about it. Just that you would get what you asked for."

"It wasn't right. It wasn't what I wanted."

"It rarely ever is." He smiled, turned, and started walking back to his car.

"You lied to me. You said I would be free, free of my family. I could start over. I could do what I wanted."

The man in his suit and smile paused, his smile broadening. It's these moments that he loves. He turned and faced James.

"See, you said it yourself. You wanted to do something." He smiles his warmest smile, the one with the most teeth but less bite. "Obviously, there was a misunderstanding about your contract, so let's examine it. You paced around this very spot swearing that she was a manipulative bitch and you never wanted kids. You said she tricked you. You said you wished they were gone so you could be free. Is that not correct?"

He allowed a small bit of bite to his smile.

"I never said that I wanted them dead. I never said that I wanted to kill them."

"Didn't you? Really?" in the air beside the two men a filmy form took shape and James was staring at himself screaming. He heard himself scream that he wished he could just end them and not get caught.

"That… that's not what I said. That's not what I meant. You tricked me." James pointed an accusing finger toward the Judge whose smile widened.

"Oh, I didn't trick you, James. In fact, I gave you exactly what you wanted. Those were not your words; however, they were your thoughts." The Judge walked slowly up to James and placed his hand on his shoulder. "You stabbed your wife. How many times?"

James didn't answer.

Beside the Judge a mass began to form. It grew steadily thicker until a man with a broad-brimmed fedora stood with a black book in his hands.

"Sir, I am Mr. October. There are a total of 36 stab wounds."

The Judge's smile held genuine glee now as he turned back to James. "How did it feel? Come on, be honest. How did it feel to pin that screaming nuisance to the crib like a bug?"

James' mouth opened to answer, but nothing came out.

"James! Really not one word?" The Judge relished the look in James' eyes. It's perfectly exquisite. "And as I promised, you will not get caught." He glanced at the man in the hat. "Your services are no longer required." The man crumpled, falling forward into a mass of black flies.

The Judge turned and opened his car door. Over his shoulder as he closed the door, he said, "James. You have a fine evening."

Within seconds the car roared into the dark, and leaving James is standing alone in the dark.

Stanley Robertson had stayed late at the Ol' Scratch Tavern, telling the same stories to anyone who would listen and drinking a few beers. He had stumbled into the night, happy, and headed for his farm. He had driven this route so many times he felt that his rusted 63 Ford half ton knew the way home on its own. With his head half out of the window, singing along with a Merle Haggard song on the radio at the top of his lungs, he rumbled down the road. His dog Jack, asleep on the seat beside him.

As he approached the crossroads, his voice quieted. He didn't want to wake the devil. As he always did, he quickly crossed his chest and held his breath. He didn't want to breathe in any dark spirits. The truck grumbled as he pushed a bit harder on the gas. A thump, a grunt and the truck bounced to a squealing stop.

Stanley sat squeezing the steering wheel, breathing hard. He didn't want to get out of the truck, didn't want to see what he had run over. Most of all, he didn't want to step foot on the crossroad. It was well past midnight, but it was dark.

Metal creaked as he slowly opened the door and stepped onto the tarmac. He walked back, hands out slightly bent, moving with cautious, hesitant steps. In the gloom, he could see a shadowy shape in the middle of the crossroads. He paused, straining to see, reluctant to get too close. He took two more steps forward. His hand reached out as if to touch the shadow, even though he was yards away.

The shape resolved itself into a man. Stanley raced forward; hands extended to the man lying in the centre of the crossroads. Stanley skidded to a stop, wanting to help, afraid to touch. Fear rose in him. Unsure of what to do. Frozen in a rising sea of panic.

Hearing footsteps on the pavement approaching in the dark, Stanley saw a man striding toward them. He took a step back.

"Good evening Mr. Peterson. How are you this fine evening?" The voice was deep, resonant, and perfectly calm.

Stanley backed up further with slow, careful steps.

"Now Judge. I don't want nothing. I ain't looking to deal no how." he said.

"Ha, no I'm not the Judge, Mr. Peterson. You may call me Mr. White, and I am not here for you."

The man lying on the pavement sat up, looked around blinking.

Stanley's truck, still idling, staggered, and nearly quit. It snapped him from his stunned stupor. He spun, ran to his truck, and jumped in. Grinding his gears, he finally found first gear, slipped the clutch, and after a hesitation he roared down the road.

"What…what happened? I was talking with The Judge. I had a deal." he rose, looking around confused. As he turned, he noticed the body on the ground, his body. "I don't understand. What's this?" He pointed at the body on the pavement.

"Well, James, you're dead."

"DEAD! I can't be. I have a deal." he looked at the tall man accusingly.

"Well, yes, you did. Now, like I said, you are dead, so your contract is complete. All that remains is to deliver you to.. Well, you know."

"But that's not the deal. I was supposed to get away from it all. I was supposed to be free."

"In the right light, some would say you are free, James." Mr. White smiled. "Shall we go?"

"Go? NO, I want to talk with The Judge."

"I believe you will be speaking with him very soon. You are going to his home." He gestured for James to follow.

James stepped toward Mr. White with some hesitation. "What will hell be like?"

Mr. White turned and looked at him. "Hell? Well, it's different for everyone, of course." he turned and started walking. James followed a pace back. "It depends on what you believe. It will look like what you expect it to. If you have visions of fire and demons with pitchforks, then that's what you will experience. For you, I do think he will have something interesting planned."

"I'm not sure I like the sound of that." he stopped walking.

"Come now. You sold your soul for a want. A single desire. How can you now think there will be no cost?"

"I never got what I asked for." he said flatly.

"Ha. You can't begin to imagine how many times I have heard those very words. No one feels like they got what they asked for and yet what they don't ever understand is that what you ask for is not what is in your heart. His game, his pleasure, is to give you your secret hidden desire. One you consciously wouldn't know about."

"I asked to be free. Nothing more."

"Free? You asked to be free? Free from what?"

"From my life. From the horrid trap I was in. I couldn't stand being a husband and a father. I felt strangled. I had no room for me. No room for what I wanted. I couldn't breathe."

"So, killing them was your way out, your way to freedom?"

"I never wanted to kill them. I just wanted to escape."

"But kill them you did." Mr. White smiled. "Quite effectively as well."

"I… I… I did what I needed to do." James said. "I had to do it." "Had to? Or wanted to? He knows you better than you yourself. When you plunged the knife into your wife, your son, and your young daughter, was that not what you wanted?"

"No, I just wanted to be free."

"Tell me James. What did you feel when you slew your family?"

"I was horrified."

"No, James, truly what went through your heart when you impaled your daughter to her crib?"

James stared into the dark, taking in the stars, the faraway lights. He smelt the dry summer fields, the slight tang of the cow pastures, and heard the soft careful sounds of the night and its creatures. He thought back and knew.

"Joy." He said quietly.

Mr. White nodded. "Yes… it is not easy to know yourself. I imagine this knowledge would be hard to accept."

"I am not a monster!"

"A monster? Oh no, you are not. In fact, you are exactly what you were meant to be."

"I don't know what that means."

"No, I suppose not." Mr. White stepped forward toward the opening. "Come." he said.

James followed.

"You have to realise. His power to manipulate the world is more about timing and a very sharp understanding of the human creature. He knew what you truly craved and knew when to push a specific button on you."

They were walking on a black sand riverbank. Overhead, James could see stars, though he didn't recognize any of the constellations. Far off there were the shapes of mountains.

"If I don't believe in hell, or heaven for that matter. Where would I go?"

They walked for several paces before Mr. White said, "Well, that's difficult to say. I imagine it would have to be as painful as he could imagine and, believe me, he knows how to be cruel. It's his nature."

In the distance, James noticed a pier with a massive boat moored at it. It reflected in the glassy surface of the black sluggish river.

"I see your boat is ready for you."

"My boat? What do you mean?"

Mr. White smiled, "Come now, James, you know where you are and what's happening. This isn't a surprise."

They walked out onto the heavy wooden pier, their steps echoing deep and hollow.

James walked a few paces alongside Mr. White. He slowed as they approached a gang plank that bridged the gap from the pier to the deck of the ship. James peered up and down the length of the large boat, noticing the dark timbers, noticing their age and weight. There was no one onboard. He looked back at Mr. White. "How does the boat move? There's no one here."

"Oh, Jean will be along when the time is right." Mr. White paused. "James, a bit of advice. Leave as much as you can behind. The more you carry with you, the harder it will be for you."

"Leave what behind?" He said, confused.

"Everything." Mr. White's smile softened a fraction. Then it returned.

James turned from the boat to respond, but he was alone on the dock. He looked around, out across the sand and the black river, then up at the pin lights above him. He walked down the gangplank, keenly aware of his booming steps on the rough wood. Once on the deck, he walked to the centre of the ship and considered the pure beauty of its simple construction. Completely unadorned with any unnecessary ornamentation, only the skillful craftsmanship.

At the gunwale, he leaned out, looking down at the shifting water. He was surprised how far down the surface was. His tiny, reflected face looked back at him. He watched the face, his face for several moments. He did not like what he saw there. That was the face of a killer. He tore his eyes away, looked up and was surprised he was not docked but was nearly across the river. At the helm stood the silhouette of a tall, dark figure draped in shadowy robes. This was the pilot. Jean was the boatman.

As he stood watching the pilot, a realisation rushed over him. He was in hell. This is what the hell was. The boat ground against the pier as it came to a stop.

James walked slowly across the deck, up the plank, and onto the pier. As soon as his feet touched the dock, the boat groaned low and deep and pulled away, returning to the far shore.

He turned and watched the boat slip easily back across the river, leaving almost no ripple in the black water. James was surprised how fast the boat traversed the distance. Within a few minutes, it was nearly at the midway point.

He started down the pier, his footfalls making a hollow, echoing sound. He felt no fear, just a mild anxiety, a fluttering in his stomach at the unknown he was facing.

Ahead, the pier ended at the dark sand, beaten flat and hard by thousands of feet. It made a distinct road as wide as the dock that vanished into the blackness. When his foot touched the sand, he was surprised it wasn't as hard packed as he imagined. His steps sank slightly into the sandy surface. However, when he happened to glance back at the boat now at the other side, he noticed the marks his passing made in the sand vanished almost as soon as his foot lifted from the surface.

As he walked, he noticed along the sides of the path he followed lay partially covered by cold black sand was a scattering of objects. Most were buried deep, so only a portion stood proud of the surface. These he could only guess at but the other objects were as confusing as they were obvious. Mostly suitcases, large and small. Some closed, others gaping open. Their contents scattered about.

Strewn among the suitcases were cellphones by the hundreds. New and old, cast aside by the multitudes that had walked this path before him. Useless artefacts from a life now over like the possessions in the suitcases.

There were other things littered amongst the refuse. Fractured scraps of white that stood out starkly against the black. With a small start, he realised the fragments were pieces of skulls, small skulls. They were the skulls of children who had been discarded along with the detritus.

Now aware of them, he looked down the road, and they stood out in stark horror.

He stared at the grisly sight. This is what people gave away in death. These are the things they left behind.

Mr. White's words came back to him. What was he going to leave behind? What would he not carry into his death?

"Down to hell," he said to the still dark air.

He couldn't think of anything he would leave behind. He had nothing that weighed on him, nothing he regretted, no dark stain to cleanse.

He straightened, glanced back to the bridge, turned his back to the past, to his life, and turned to face his new existence.

He started walking forward, ready. A few steps and his toe caught on something, a stone, or a stick. He stumbled, falling forward. His arms flew forward to catch himself. His palms ground painfully on the coarse sand. He pushed himself over to a sitting position and brushed his hands off.

After a second, he looked at what had tripped him and ruined his triumphant walk into hell.

With a wry smile, he saw it was a small broken skull bleached white, half buried in the black sand.

With a chuckle, he stood in the darkness. Confused, he looked around, unsure of where he was. The road, the bridge, even the river and the fall off mountains were gone.

With an uneasy realization, he knew exactly where he was and when.

Hesitantly, he moved forward to the light that came down the hallway of his home.

Like in a dream, he watched his hand reach forward to open his baby daughter's bedroom door.

Absently, he noticed his hands were wet and dripped redly. The door slid open quietly.

Inside, he could hear his own voice repeating a single word. A chant in the dream he was trapped in.

He walked up to the crib and looked down at the tiny sleeping body. The smell of that small life, sweat and warmth, washed over him.

He placed both hands on the crib's edge, gripping it until his knuckles turned white even through the gore that covered both his hands and the brutal hunting knife he held.

Inside, he screamed the single word mantra as he watched, helpless to stop it.

The blade plunged down through the small rib cage to bury itself into the thin mattress below.

Once, twice and a third time. He left the knife there jutting obscenely from the still form, all the while he screamed.

He turned from the ghastly scene and stiffly walked to the door, reached for the brass doorknob and opened it. He walked into his daughter's bedroom, all the while screaming.

He walked up to the sleeping child. He grasped the crib's sides, his hand dripping with gore. His daughter slept, lost in her own tiny dreams. He watched the little chest rise and fall in a warm, safe rhythm.

He raised his hand up. Raised the knife above the tiny body and watched, detached as it plunged down, again and again and again.

He turned from the shattered body, the handle of the knife jutting accusingly from the broken, bloody body.

He walked toward the door, reached down to the doorknob, and knew he had arrived in his own hell. He would relive this moment in time forever.

As he raised the knife, he continued to scream, silent and desperate, "NO NO NO NO NO NO NO NO NO NO NO NO NO NO NO NO NO NO NO NO NO NO NO NO NO NO NO NO NO NO NO NO NO NO NO NO NO NO NO NO NO NO NO NO NO NO NO NO NO NO NO NO NO NO NO NO NO NO NO NO NO NO NO NO NO NO NO NO!"

Something shifted. It must be the failing light. She looked taller.

6

PASSING IT FORWARD

Originally published in A Lead Pill

Usually, all ten of the motel's windows facing Highway 11 had the drapes closed tight against the headlights of westbound cars that glared straight into those rooms making it nearly impossible to sleep. There weren't many cars passing. This stretch of blacktop was rarely used, but even one could ruin a night's sleep.

Glen stood in the frozen gravel drive off Highway 11, his back to the motel, looking into the dark forest across the highway. Behind him, a single light on a pole lit the parking area. It cast a long shadow in front of him into the dark.

He considered his breath as it frosted in the night air. It mixed with the smoke from his cigarette. He took a drag, then flicked the butt into the dark and watched the glowing tip vanish. His jacket was open, despite the cold. He could feel its bite on his nose and fingertips.

He looked into the sky above him. He was always amazed at how many stars he could see here. In the city there were stars, but here there were a thousand times more. Tonight however, the sky was dark. The stars were nowhere to be seen and the full moon shone weakly through heavy cloud cover.

He turned and looked at the motel. The motel must have been sitting here for over 40 years, maybe longer, and it showed. He had started working here when he had dropped out of college. He didn't want to go back home and hear the disappointment in his mother's voice again. A friend in his dorm had said he knew of a job that would pay OK, and it would give him a quiet place to consider what he was going to do next.

It certainly gave him time to think. Every night for the past three months, he sat at the desk and read and thought and smoked. He wasn't any closer to an idea than the day he'd arrived. He had begun to believe this had been a bad idea. This motel had started to feel like a prison, like a place he would never escape.

It wasn't a busy motel. Many nights, he had not one stop. A person had to be pretty tired to stop here. It wasn't welcoming. It needed paint. The office window was cracked, with a small sliver of glass missing. Years ago, someone had taped the hole over with masking tape. The tape had all but disintegrated.

'Motel' written in big block letters on the roof, had a horror movie feel. Many of the bulbs that shone up at the wooden painted letters were burnt out or on their last days. The tiny neon 'office' sign was barely visible.

He looked at the single black window. It reminded him of a missing tooth. It was the second to last window. It was room nine. He wanted to go and check, yet he also did not want to. He was unsure of what he would find. He would have to check soon, but not yet. He stared at the black window. With an animal shake he walked back to his office.

He sat in his chair and stared out the window. Nights were quiet. He had been on the nightshift from day one. The owner of the motel had asked if he was OK with the night shift. Glen had said it was perfect. He needed time to think. The man had laughed, "Well, you'll get plenty of time for that," and hired him.

Glen pulled out his Jack Reacher novel that he had found in a used bookstore. It was dog-eared and had cost him a buck. He had read it before but enjoyed the security of a world where one man could be that sure, that untroubled by anything. He read and reread the same paragraph, and in frustration, he put the book down. He leaned back in his chair. It creaked and threatened to tip over backwards. He was doing his best not to think about room nine, not to think about what was in there.

He sat for as long as he could. He put the 'Back in a minute' sign on the window and walked down the building. He stood looking at the door with the 9 on it.

He knocked lightly, then opened the door. It was dark in the room except for the light that came in from the yard.

"Hello?" he whispered to the dark. There was no response. The bathroom door opened, and light flooded out. A dream walked out, carried by the light. He stared; his mouth open. She was a vision, a vision out of his deepest fantasy.

The woman stood, unselfconsciously naked except for a towel around her head. She smiled at him.

"Hello," she said. She pulled the towel off and bent forward to dry her hair.

"Are you OK?" he asked.

"I'm fine. Much better, thank you, and thank you for letting me stay here."

"Humm, no problem," he said, "I don't have any clothes that would fit you, but I brought you a pair of coveralls."

"Oh, thank you. That's great." She stepped forward and took the rolled-up bundle. They were used and smelled of oil and varsol. She unrolled the coveralls, stepped into the legs, and pulled them over her shoulders.

He should look away. He shouldn't stare, but he couldn't pull away. He was mesmerized.

Her ribs pushed up and forward as she pulled her arms into the sleeves. She bent and rolled up the long pant legs, first one leg, then the other. Once done, she stood straight and started rolling up the sleeves. The zipper still undone opened; one breast teased him as it popped in and out of view.

Once her sleeves were rolled up, she pulled the zipper up to her neck. He felt a pang of loss.

"You should close the curtains," he said, pointing at them.

She looked at him, puzzled and said, "OK." She walked past him and closed the curtains.

"Do you need anything? Are you hungry?" he asked.

"No, I don't think so," she responded. Again, the puzzled look.

"You look a lot better," he said.

"I do?"

Now it was his turn to look puzzled.

He remembered how he had found her. He had slipped out back for a smoke, and she had been laying in the snow. The snow was stained red from the blood. Her clothing was shredded and was mostly torn away as was her flesh. She was drenched with blood.

He was sure she was dead, then her eyes flashed open. He went to her. He didn't know what to do. She looked bad. He reached for her but stopped, afraid to touch her.

"It's OK. I'll call an ambulance."

"NO!" she said and had grabbed his hand with such force it had hurt.

"But you're hurt!" he said looking around, trying to decide what to do.

"It's not as bad as it looks. I just need a place to clean up and maybe sleep," she said. She rolled slightly to her left and pushed herself upright. He rushed forward and helped her to her feet. She was tiny. He held her up and walked her to the closest room.

He opened the room and switched on the light. She flinched and screamed, "NO, no light."

"OK, OK," he said, turning the light off. He had seen her though, in that brief light, had seen deep gashes across her back and chest that were still bleeding. She was cut up pretty badly.

He winced as he lay her down on the bed, partly from the pain it caused her and partly from the blood that was certainly going to be soaking into the bedding. He wasn't sure how he was going to explain that.

She whimpered, curled into a fetal pose, and fell asleep. He stood, looking at her. He really should call the cops or something. This was nuts. He was in so much trouble. Her hand reached out and grasped his.

"Thank you. Just a little time. It will all be OK," she said.

She held his hand. He stood still for a long time, her hand slipped as she fell into a deeper sleep. He watched her breathing. It was rhythmic and steady. He turned and left for a smoke.

Remembering this, he exclaimed, "You were all cut up when I found you."

She looked at him, "Oh, that. It looked far worse than it was," she smiled.

"It looked pretty bad. You had very deep gashes on your back and your chest. I saw them," he said, suddenly not as sure as he had been a few minutes ago.

"Well, you just saw me," she smiled, tipping her head down slightly, "I looked alright, didn't I?"

"Yes," he said, blushing.

She smiled, enjoying his discomfort. She sat on the edge of the bed.

"What happened to you?" he asked.

Her smile slipped, then returned as bright as ever.

"Oh, it was a misunderstanding. My father..."

"Wait! Your dad did that to you?" he said, shocked.

"No... well, not really," she looked down at her hands, "It was not his fault."

"What do you mean? Did he do this?"

"Well, what he did, he didn't know he did. He didn't know what he gave me, and that was a while ago. 'Sides, he bit a lead pill a couple of months back, so it's not important anymore," she laughed lightly, "I guess it wasn't lead. A silver pill then," she smiled at her private joke.

He looked at her, baffled by how she could defend her dad if he was responsible for what he had seen.

"Glen, right?" She stood and moved close to him.

"Um, yes, Glen," he said.

She moved closer still, "I need you to help me, Glen." She put her hand on his chest, "I need a place to stay for a couple of days."

"I...you can't stay here. I'm sorry. My shift ends at six."

"I just need a couple of days. Can I come home with you?" She slid her arm up and around his neck, "Just a couple of days."

"It's not much," he said, thinking about the small house he rented. It was tiny.

"It will be perfect," she pulled him down to her and kissed him.

"I guess you can come," he mumbled.

She kissed him again, jumped, wrapped her legs around him.

He returned her smile.

"But first I have to clean up this room," he said, looking about.

"I can help," she said brightly.

The comforter was soaked with blood. There was a single small barefoot print in blood on the carpet. He wasn't sure what he was going to do about that, but the comforter and the sheets he could replace from the storeroom. He couldn't leave them with laundry. There would be questions. He would take them home, wash them at his laundromat and return them clean.

He looked at her. He realized he didn't know her name. "What's your name?"

She laughed, "Christine, Christine Rutland. Nice to meet you." She extended her small hand. He smiled and shook it.

"You stay here, Christine. It's too cold to be traipsing around in bare feet. I'll go and get clean bedding," he said.

He hesitated, wondering if leaving her alone was such a good idea, then–still unsure–turned and left. The storeroom was behind the office. He walked through the cold, unlocked the storeroom, and pulled the chain to turn the light on. He had to slide around the maid's cart to the bedding. He pulled down sheets, pillowcases, and a comforter. He pulled the chain, locked the door, and walked back. He glanced at his watch. Still an hour before his shift ended.

He opened the door to nine and stopped. Christine was on her hands and knees in the middle of the floor. At first, he could not figure out what she was doing, then he saw. She was licking the bloody footprint.

"What...?" he asked. He couldn't believe what he was seeing.

She sat back on her heels and smiled at him. She wiped her mouth with a hand.

"I've just about got it all," she said with pride.

He looked at the carpet. She was right, it was gone. "Gross," he thought, "but it worked."

Slightly shaken, he moved to the bed and pulled the comforter off. Christine rose and helped. It was done in minutes. Glen rolled up the bloody bedding.

"Stay here. I'll be right back," he said.

"Oh, just a sec," she ran to the bathroom and came back holding what remained of her clothes.

"Don't forget these." She held them out with two fingers and screwed up her nose. He took the blood-soaked rags, once again marvelling at how much blood she had lost yet had no wounds on her at all.

He took the bedding and rags to his truck and tossed them into the box. He leaned on the truck. This wasn't right. He looked up at the sky, looking for stars, but saw only black. A quick glance at his watch. Dave would be here soon to take over. He climbed into the truck and started it. It took a couple of turns before it fired but then roared to life. He turned the heater on high and closed the door, letting it idle.

He walked back to the room. Christine was sitting on the bed. She looked up when he came in and smiled. Glen looked around the room. It looked OK.

"Dave will be here soon. I'll take you to the truck. It'll be warm. You can wait there," he said.

"OK," she said and stood.

"Your feet will freeze. I'll carry you." He stepped forward. She smiled at him and put her arms around his neck, "OK," she whispered.

He picked her up easily and carried her to his truck. She opened the door, and he lifted her to the truck seat. It wasn't warm, but it was getting there.

He had closed the truck door and started walking to the office when he saw headlights on the highway. The car slowed, signalled, and turned into the parking lot. It was Dave, slightly early as always. He pulled his Ford up to the office, shut it off and stepped out.

"Morning," Glen said.

Dave looked at him, frowned, "Morning."

Dave wasn't a morning person. He needed several cups of coffee and about an hour to come alive.

"Nothing has changed. Only those two guys from the plant in 11 and 12," Glen said.

"K," Dave responded as he walked to the office, Glen following. Glen watched Dave hang up his coat, sit and adjust things the way he liked them. He handed Glen his dog-eared paperback with a look of distaste.

"Ok. Have a good morning," Dave said.

"You too," Glen said as he left the office.

Glen walked to his truck, his boots squeaking in the snow. It always seemed colder just before dawn. The cab was warm when he climbed in. Christine smiled at him. She waited till he had settled into his seat, then she slid across the seat to sit right beside him. It made him feel special.

The truck was an old standard Chev with the long stick that stood straight from the floorboards. He pulled the stick back into reverse. His fingers stroked her thigh. She pushed forward into his fingers. His body reacted like he had never felt before. For a second, he was flustered, confusion washing over him.

He shook slightly and pushed the truck into first and pulled out onto the highway.

Glen had rented a cabin not far from the motel. They were only a few minutes on the highway when Christine pulled her legs up, slid down her head in Glen's lap and fell asleep. Overwhelmed by the coveralls, she looked like a child. Glen looked at her quiet, sleeping face. He felt a swell of a feeling he was unfamiliar with. He needed to protect her. He needed to keep her safe.

When he got to the cabin, she was still asleep. He picked her up easily and carried her into the cabin. The cabin was usually rented to hunters and ice fishermen in the winter months, and in the summer to families on vacation. It was small, but it had all he needed: a kitchen, a bedroom, and a bathroom with a shower. It didn't have much in the way of hot water, but enough. In the main room was a small potbelly stove.

He put her down on the old blue couch and set to lighting a fire in the stove. The cabin warmed quickly. He made his bed, then sat down beside her on the couch to wait for her to wake.

He woke in bed. A sliver of sunlight edged his heavy curtains. He stretched, then jumped when a soft voice said, "Afternoon, sleepyhead. You want a coffee?"

He sat up, the night before flooding back. Christine sat at the edge of his bed, smiling.

"Ya, a coffee would be great."

Christine stood and skipped out of the room. She was wearing one of his sweaters. It hung off one shoulder and halfway down to her knees.

She came back in a minute, smiling, carrying a mug. He took it in both hands.

"Thank you," he said, "I musta been very tired. I don't remember comin' to bed."

"Oh, honey. When I woke, you were passed out. You looked so cute." She touched his cheek, "So I put you to bed."

"I don't remember," he sipped on his coffee.

"You never woke. I carried you in and tucked you in."

He looked down, noticing he was naked under the covers.

"Ya, I tucked you in. I thought you would be more comfortable without all those tight clothes." She grinned, as he looked down. Her eyes looked at him from under her eyebrows. There was mischief in those eyes.

"You undressed me?" he asked.

"After I carried you in here," she smiled, her head coming up.

"Wait. What do you mean, 'You' carried me?"

"I'm stronger than I look," she said proudly.

He looked at her, surprised.

She leaned forward. The sweater hung open, revealing her small breasts. He looked. She smiled as she took his coffee, placed it on the night table, and pulled the sweater over her head.

She stood in front of him naked. He looked at her. Inside, he laughed at himself. Here is this gorgeous woman standing naked in front of him, and he's looking for half-healed cuts

or scars. There was nothing. Her skin was perfect. She was
perfect.

Christine climbed into bed, pushing him back and down.

"See? Nothing. Not a scratch. I heal quick." she said and
kissed him.

When he woke, he was alone. The slit at the side of his
curtain showed nothing but dark. He glanced at his watch. It
was after 8.

"Christine?" he called. He pushed the sheets down and
went to the bathroom. While he was pissing, he caught his
reflection in the vanity mirror. He had long scratches down
his back. He reached around, touched them, winced, and
smiled at how he had gotten them.

"Christine?" He called louder this time. He walked around
the small cabin looking for her, knowing she was gone.
Somewhere deep inside himself, a little thing broke like a tiny
spring that he never knew existed, suddenly gave under a
lifetime of strain.

He walked to the window and pushed open the curtain.
He looked at the snow-draped forest in the semi-dark. He
stood till the sun had set and he could see the reflection of
his naked pale body. He looked at himself. He was just a man,
nothing special. She was special, out of this world special. A
being so pure it could never belong to someone like him.

He turned from the window and got dressed. It would
soon be time to go to work. But it wasn't. He had hours to wait

and nothing to fill them with. He sat on his couch as the cabin cooled. The fire had died long ago. He knew he should restart the fire. He knew he should eat something. He sat staring at nothing, until it was time to go.

He pulled on his coat and boots and trudged to the truck. He groaned when he realized he had forgotten to plug it in. The truck barely turned over. At first, he was sure it wouldn't start but finally with a roar it came to life. His breath white in the cab, he drove to the motel and fell into his routine. His shift passed without excitement.

On his drive home, an idea popped into his mind. Maybe she's there waiting for me.

He pushed hard on the accelerator. His old truck growled as it shifted down. He skidded into the campsite and stopped in front of his cabin, threw the truck door open and raced to the door. Inside, it was cold and dark. She was not there.

He stood in the middle of the room. He walked to the couch and sat. After a couple of minutes, he laid down. His coat still on, he pulled his booted feet up on the couch and fell asleep.

"Glen?" The voice was a man's, coming from outside. Glen heard it. He ignored it. He was tired. He just needed to sleep.

"Glen?" The voice was closer, then the voice was right beside him.

"Glen! What the fuck! Your gonna freeze!" he yelled, shaking Glen. He pulled Glen to a sitting position, "Wake up!"

"I'm tired. Just let me sleep," Glen said or thought he had. It came out as unintelligible mumbles.

"Glen! Wake up!" the man yelled again. He shook Glen. "Fuck! Ah gotta warm you up!"

He rushed to the stove, slamming the door shut as he passed. He got the fire burning, went to the kitchen and turned on the elements and oven, leaving the oven door open. He raced around the cottage, opening the curtains to let in the sunlight.

Glen had slid back down to a prone position. The man sat him upright again.

"Glen! Wake up! You can't sleep now!" the man yelled.

Glen tried to push the man away. He felt drunk, his movements clumsy. The man slapped him across the face, hard. His eyes popped open, startled.

"What..?" Glen managed to say.

It took some work, but the man finally got Glen on his feet. He stumbled around with the man's arms helping. They walked till the man was sweating and Glen was moving on his own. The cabin was warm.

Glen recognized his saviour. It was Sam, the old guy he had rented the cabin from.

"I saw yer truck with the door open, then I saw the cabin door open too. What the fuck were you thinking?" Sam asked.

Glen looked at Sam, "I was just tired. It was a long shift."

"Well, pretty fucking stupid," he said. He looked around the cabin. "Ok, you ok?"

"Ya, I'm good. Thank you," Glen said. Sam grunted and left. Glen shut off the stove and oven. He undressed, had a warm shower till the water became cold, crawled into bed, and went to sleep.

It was night when he woke. He hadn't drawn the curtains, and the blackness surrounded the cabin. He slipped out of bed, hugged himself against the chill of the air and put some wood in the stove. It was down to embers, but it got burning quickly.

He went to the window to look at the stars through the trees. He could see very few because the moon, full and bright, dominated the sky. He looked at the moon, it seemed so close. In the cold night air, it had an intensity that seemed to almost have a heat to it. He felt a pull to it like vertigo.

A shape caught his eye as he was looking up. It crossed the yard between the cabin and his truck. The moonlight outlined the shape. He wasn't sure what it was, an animal, maybe a dog or bear. It was dark, fur-covered and moved quickly past the truck into the trees where it vanished. It could have been anything. He was living in the boonies.

He turned back to the room. He checked his watch. It was nearly time to go to work. He crossed the floor, dressed, pulled on his coat and boots.

Outside, he looked for tracks in the snow. He found too many to decipher anything from them.

Once again, he had forgotten to plug the truck in. He turned the ignition and was rewarded with a dull click. He tried a couple more times. He was going to need a boost. He plugged the truck in knowing it wouldn't do much good at this point, and if he wasn't going to be late, he'd have to walk over to Sam's. Late as it was, he hoped Sam was in, awake, and willing to come out to give him a boost.

His feet crunched on the cold hard-packed snow. He shoved his hands deep in his pockets, hunched over against the cold. The hairs in his nose seemed to freeze. It took a few minutes to get to Sam's. Glen was happy to see that the house was lit up.

A noise off to his right in the trees made him turn. Something was following him, walking in the deep snow there. He walked faster. The footfalls didn't speed up, but neither did they stop.

He was nearly running by the time he got to Sam's front door. Whatever was pacing him had stopped, he could no longer hear it in the trees. He knocked on Sam's door and heard Sam curse from inside. The door flew open, Sam stood in the doorway glaring but softened when he recognized Glen.

"Oh, it's you. You OK?" Sam asked.

"Yes, I'm good. Thanks again. That was stupid," Glen said.

"It sure the fuck was," Sam said, "What do you need?"

"I'm sorry to bug you with this but my truck. I didn't plug it in so..."

"So, you need a boost. OK, no problem. Step inside while I get my coat an' boots on." Sam turned from the door, leaving it open for Glen to walk in. He followed, glancing behind at the trees. He didn't see anything.

Sam's house was nothing like his cabins, it was a real home. From where Glen stood watching Sam pull his jacket on, he could see Sam's wife. He couldn't remember her name. The room she was in was dark except for the glow of the TV.

"I'm going to give Glen a boost," Sam called out.

"K. Is he OK?" Sam's wife asked.

"I'm good, thanks," Glen said.

"I'm glad to hear it. Stay warm,"

"Back in a sec," Sam said as he opened the door to his right that led to the garage. Glen followed, closing the door behind him.

It only took a minute to drive back to Glen's truck. Sam nosed in tight to it. They got out, opened their hoods and hooked up the cables that Sam had pulled from behind the seat. Glen climbed into the cab and the engine started after a few tries. He left it idling, jumped out to help but Sam had the cables unhooked and rolled up already.

"Thanks, Sam. You're a lifesaver."

"Yup, more than once," Sam smiled. "Don't make it ah habit."

"No'ser. I won't," Glen chuckled.

Glen climbed into the cab of his truck as Sam drove away. It was already warming up. He drove to work, his mind on Christine. He had so many questions. He couldn't stop thinking about her.

He got to the motel and settled into his shift. He picked up his book again. He put it down when he had reread the same paragraph three times and still couldn't remember what it was about. He just couldn't concentrate. He stared into the night and shivered. It was so cold and dark. To be out in that, alone and hurt. It terrified him.

Something moved just out of sight, a slightly less dark shape against the black. He stood and looked harder. There was something there.

He pulled his coat on, grabbed a flashlight, and walked outside. He pointed the flashlight's beam into the black past the parking lot's light. It found nothing. He kept moving forward till he reached the edge of the light. The flashlight beam pushed against the dark.

Two red dots in the black. He stared, not knowing what he was looking at, then the red dots blinked. Glen stepped back a pace. The red eyes stared at him, steadily, calmly. He took another step backwards. From the dark, he heard a low growl. So low, so slow it was a series of bass note clicks. He stopped.

He realized that the animal he was looking at was either very large or in a tree. The eyes were more than a head taller than himself. He hoped it was in a tree. The growl came again, so low he felt it rather than heard it. He stepped backwards.

The creature stepped forward, the moonlight catching the top of its head. It was not a small creature in a tree. Its large triangular head could just be seen. It had very tall, pointed ears with tufts of hair at the tips making them look even taller, thinner.

He stood still, eyes wide, mouth agape. When the growl came again, he turned and ran.

He ran flat out like a hound from hell was on his tail... and maybe it was. He tripped in the middle of the parking lot. He fell hard skidding on the frozen gravel. He rolled onto his back, expecting fangs to snatch at him, claws to tear at him.

Nothing. No claws, no fangs, and no red eyes. Only the dark.

Suddenly the air was filled with a roar, and brightness surrounded him. He crabbed backwards as a truck skidded to a stop, narrowly missing him. The driver jumped out of the truck.

"What the hell are ya doin on the ground! I damn near run ya over!" the driver yelled.

Glen looked past the driver, to the dark of the forest.

"What's wrong with you? Ya drunk or sumin?"

"No, no, sorry. Just slipped," Glen said.

"Well, it's a good way to got yer self kilt."

The black mass that flew out of the dark, smashed into the driver with such force it lifted the side of the truck up, threatening to tip it over and pushing it sideways several feet. The driver had enough time to scream once, then the inside of the truck's windshield was hosed with blood. The truck shook violently as sounds of rending and tearing, mixed with low snarling, filled the parking lot.

Glen scrambled to his feet and raced to the office. He slammed the door behind himself and grabbed the phone and dialled 911.

"This is Glen at the motel on 89. There's a wolf or a bear attacking a man in the parking lot!"

From where Glen stood, phone to his ear, only partly hearing the woman on the other end of the line saying they were sending someone, he watched the truck shake. He stopped listening completely when the truck went still. His arm sank, still holding the receiver.

From around the truck stepped a wolf, but unlike any wolf he had ever seen. It had huge hackles, long ears and a thin tapering snout. Its red eyes looked at him. It was tall, standing taller than he was, on surprisingly thin, almost delicate legs that ended in large paws. It stood still for what seemed like a long time, then its ears perked. Its lips pulled back to reveal extremely long canines. It growled low and turned to disappear into the dark trees.

Glen stood still for several minutes until he heard sirens coming down the highway. He became aware he still held the receiver at his side. He brought it to his ear. The woman was frantic.

"Yes," he said calmly and hung up.

The two cop cars came screaming into the parking lot seconds later. The blue and red flashing lights bathed the parking lot in a weird festive atmosphere. He walked out of his office, slow and calm.

"You Glen?" the young cop called.

"Yes," Glen said as he walked towards him.

"Where's the attack?"

"Yes," Glen said, pointing at the truck.

He watched two of the officers walk to the truck. They both swore when they saw what was there. One gagged but didn't throw up. The remaining two officers nervously joined them. They turned on Glen, demanding to know what happened. He told them, calm and detached, then he told them again.

More cops arrived as well as an ambulance. It was crowded.

Absently Glen thought he wasn't going to have any customers tonight. His boss would be pissed. It wasn't his fault, he thought indignantly.

He overheard one of the cops who seemed to be in charge complaining, "This is the worst fucking day! Starting with some young girl going on a killing spree with a kitchen knife. Sliced up her boyfriend, now this. I fucking hate full moons. It brings on the crazy."

Glen was asked several more times what he had seen. By the time they said he could go home, the sun was up. His boss was stomping around trying to get this mess cleaned up as soon as possible so he could get back to business. He wasn't having much luck. He didn't talk to Glen, just nodded.

Glen drove to his cabin slowly. Pulled up in front. Plugged the truck in as he walked to his door. Inside he walked straight to his bed, crawled in fully dressed and went to sleep.

It was late afternoon when he awoke to a noise. He climbed out of bed and walked into the main room. Christine sat there on the couch in his dirty, too big coveralls.

"Christine?" he said.

She looked at him. There was a sadness in her eyes, "Hi, Glen. Miss me?"

"Christine, where'd you go?"

She shook her head. "Oh, I've been around."

He wanted to go to her, to pick her up, to hold her, but something in her voice made him stay where he was.

"I'm sorry. I thought I could do it. I thought I could stay away. You are so kind, so loving, and it's not fair, but I like you." She stood, stepping towards him. "My father didn't know what he did. He thought he was doing what he had to. He was wrong, but I never got to tell him."

She stopped in the middle of the room and glanced out the window at the creeping twilight.

"I don't want to be alone. My last boyfriend wasn't nice to me when the change came over him. I fixed him earlier today."

She smiled and started to unzip the coveralls, "I want you to be with me. I'm sorry there is only one way you and I can be together."

She let the coveralls fall to the floor. She stood in the half-light, beautiful, pale and naked. Glen's eyes traced her body. He felt himself stir.

Something shifted. It must be the failing light. She looked taller. She jerked, then she bent over like she was in pain. Her long hair fell forward. The light slipped into darkness. She growled low. When she stood, two red eyes regarded him. He stood frozen, trying to understand what had just happened.

She leaped.

But the vision was spoiled. Her hands and feet were covered in mud and had smeared abstract patterns across the sheets.

7

A QUESTION OF PAYMENT

He rolled onto his back with a groan, looking at the ceiling. He really needed to take a piss, and had been holding it all the while, willing himself back to sleep, but now it had become urgent. He gave up, pushed the covers back and headed to the can. When he returned, thinking he might sleep maybe another hour or maybe more, he stopped breathless. What he saw was a vision from his earliest fantasies. Christine sprawled out face down, naked limbs cast about with careless abandon. A thought flitted through his mind. Maybe he could wake her with a kiss on the back of her neck. She would like that, but if he turned that kiss into a bite, she would make that small noise he loved, and they would spend the next hour wrapped in each other. He imagined what that could offer.

Relishing the thought, he just stood at the end of the bed, watching her, watching her breath. He took her in. Her body, slight and perfect, skin smooth, unblemished, the colour of coffee. She lay stark against the white sheets. But the vision was spoiled. Her hands and feet were covered in mud and had smeared abstract patterns across the sheets. He knows she went hunting last night without him. Disappointed, his fantasy vanished like the popping of a shiny soap bubble. He turned to the kitchen to make coffee.

He was on his second cup of coffee, sitting and staring out at the morning and the street, when he heard her moving in the bedroom. She stepped into the room, engulfed in one of his sweatshirts. It hung almost to her knees; the neck sliding off one smooth shoulder. Her long hair was a mess. She pushed at it; dried mud flaked off her fingers. She insinuated herself onto his lap, curling up into a ball like a cat. Once settled, she weighed nothing. She could feel his annoyance.

"Sorry, babe. I woke, and I just needed a nibble. I just went out back. It wasn't a hunt. Honest. It was just a rabbit."

He did not look down at her. Across the street, he could see a man in a robe staring at his phone, a rat of a dog on a pink leash. The man, still half asleep, snapped the leash in frustration, wanting the dog to be done so he could return to bed. The dog, a tiny nervous thing, vibrated with cold and fear. It had barely finished when the owner yanked the leash and stomped back up the sidewalk to a perfectly ordinary house.

Glen felt sorry for the dog, even a bit embarrassed for it. Inside his chest, he growled.

"Don't be mad." She said, misunderstanding. "It was just a rabbit."

He looked down, not understanding at first, then he realised. A half-smile touched the corners of his lips.

Her face beamed with a smile with bright white teeth. Relieved she snuggled into him, she said, "A very tiny rabbit."

"How about we go for breakfast?" he said and stood, dropping her on the ground. She landed with a thump.

"Hey.."

He reached down and took her hand, lifting to her feet with ease.

"Well?"

"Ya, breakfast sounds good. I'm starving."

"Starving?"

"It was a very small rabbit. I told you," She said.

"Small"

"Very."

"Ha. Ok, where do you want to go?"

"Hummm? How about the Moon? I feel like pancakes." She skipped to the bedroom to get dressed.

"You always feel like pancakes," he said absently, looking across the street at the house where the neighbour and his little dog entered.

The moon was an uber cool breakfast joint with a retro feel and amazing food run by these two stunning blondes. They were a couple, but they had a string of would-be suitors sitting at the bar day after day.

Glen and Christine never missed a Saturday brunch, even on a cycle day. They just made it work.

It was always mad busy, but they were patient and got a table in short order. Glen smiled at the server as she put the menu down, already knowing what they would want.

"Morning. The usual?" She leaned on one hip and glanced across the restaurant to the full patio.

"Ha ya same as ever," Glen said. Christine looked up from her phone and nodded with a smile.

"You got it." She left and returned with coffee.

"I think I want to head north today. I have a hankering for something wild." Glen said after a couple of sips. Christine hummed, "Ah ya sure. That sounds good."

Glen watched her for a second. She didn't look up, still completely engrossed in her phone. He ground his teeth together; jaw clenched so tight it squeaked.

"I know. I know. Just a sec," with exaggerated movements, she carefully placed the phone on the table and smiled big and cartoonish. "Happy?"

"Yes. Thank you." He reached for his coffee, ignoring her.

Glen caught a scent wrapped in the smell of coffee, egg, and fried bacon. At first, he couldn't place it. It was just a scent slightly out of place, but there, definitely there. A scent as he focused on it, he recognized, though he had never smelled it before. It was familiar in a way he couldn't describe.

Christine was going on about what she had read online, the hilarious cat video she had seen and examined her nails considering a new colour. Then, in the middle of a sentence, she stopped.

"There's one here." She whispered, leaning forward.

Glen looked at her and knew.

"Are you sure?" He asked.

She nodded, slow and deliberate, looking around the restaurant. "Yes. Absofuckinglutly. There's one here with us."

"Do you know who it is? Can you see them?"

"No. It's not that they're all hairy and shit." She looked up at him with a sarcastic arc of her eyebrow.

"Ya ok." He said, feeling foolish. Their food came, and he glanced around the room. She laughed.

"You're not going to be able to recognize them."

"No, I suppose not." He frowned as she pulled out her phone and started taking photos of their food.

An hour later, they were on the road heading north. The traffic in the city was heavy but lightened as they got onto the highway. Glen drove leisurely. They were not in a hurry and did not have an actual destination. They would drive till just before the moon rose, then pull off the road.

Christine stayed on her phone for a while, feet on the dash, toes splayed on the windshield.

He liked the otherness of her. He liked her tiny features, liked her slim hands and delicate feet. The perfection of the girliness of her, the flawless skin. He felt privileged to be with her. He watched her feet, disappointed when she slipped her phone into her pocket, tucked her feet under her, making herself into a tiny ball and fell asleep.

Glen relaxed into the drive, watching the landscape shift. Traffic became lighter until they were the only car on the highway. He wished he had taken the roof off. It was one reason he loved owning a Jeep. When they had bought it, Christine got so excited. She loved the air rushing around her. She would push her arms up into the wind and laugh, her hair buffeting around her smiling face.

As he drove, he smiled at the memory. He glanced to the west and noticed heavy dark clouds hugging the horizon. He watched them, sensing their approach. Glen could smell the rain, could even smell the wet fields and the damp earth. Deep inside the dark mass, Glen saw the occasional flash of lightning.

Christine made a little noise, a small growl. Glen smiled. She must be hunting in her dream. He watched her eyes flash back and forth under eyelids. He glanced back at the road, checked the mirror, and saw a car far off behind them.

The hair on the back of his neck pricked. There was no reason. It was just another car, but something made him wary. He felt a growl deep in his throat.

"What's wrong?" Christine sat up and looked around.

"It's nothing." He said automatically.

"It's not nothing. Something has you riled."

"Oh, it's probably nothing. There's a car behind us."

Christine pulled herself up in her seat and looked out the car window. After a minute, "I see it." She watched the road behind. She lifted her head, closed her eyes, and breathed in. "There's a storm. Let's drive to the rain. Everything smells so much better wet."

Glen glanced to the west. The storm was closer. "Sure. That's a good idea. And we'll know if the car is following us."

She smiled. "Yes, and we can hunt in the rain. I love to hunt in the rain."

Glen turned off the highway as soon as he found an off-ramp heading west. The road was narrow, paved and hilly, lined with thick, overgrown trees. The sun cast long shadows that flashed across the hood and windshield as they drove along. Glen glanced into the mirror every few minutes, checking for the car. He did not see it until the sun had fallen below the bank of clouds. It got dark. Glen flipped on the headlights and glanced in the mirror. There were headlights behind them. There was no way of knowing if it was the same car, but inside he knew it was.

"It's there." He said.

Christine looked back down the road. "It might just be someone travelling the same direction." She looked at Glen, knowing he didn't think so.

"I'm going to turn off and see." Glen said, scanning the edge of the road looking for a spot that he could pull off.

He found an approach and slowed. He slowed, turned, and drove through the break in the trees. The car bounced across the rough field. Glen idled the car behind a dense clump of trees and parked.

"Now what? It's too early." Christine said.

Glen climbed out of the car. "Oh, it's not that early." He could feel her excitement. It radiated off her in waves, like heat. He smiled, knowing it mirrored his own. His heart was racing. It could feel it thumping in his temples.

He walked around the Jeep and pulled Christine's door open. She bounded out, wrapping her arms around his neck, and kissed him. Her tongue sliding across his teeth. When she pulled her head back, she was grinning a grin he loved. He let go of her. She dropped to the ground and started undressing.

Glen grinned and undid his pants. When he pulled his t-shirt over his head, the most magnificent sight greeted him. In the time it took him to remove his t-shirt, she had completely undressed, clothing scattered about her. Only her black bra hung on her outstretched finger. With an evil grin, she flicked the bra at him and leaped, knocking him backward. Together, they slammed into the rough earth. She straddled him, fingers digging into his hair. Her lips pressed hard against his. He wrapped his arms around her and flipped her on her back, pushing down on her with all of his weight. He ground his hips down as his erection screamed against his jeans.

Beneath him, she was pushing her hips up as she began to shift. As usual, her change started at the head, which was already engulfed in hair. Her teeth glinted in the gloom. The growl that escaped from her lips was only partially human.

With both hands on her shoulders, he pushed up and back, arching back. The rain began. Each drop, startling, crisp and sharp on his bare skin.

Her claws raked down his stomach to the waistband of his jeans, leaving shallow scratches, small beads of blood rose. The claws dug in, slicing through the fabric deeper into his flesh. The pain became exquisite as the jeans fell off him. She cut downward, blood soaking the remains of his pants. Somewhere deep in his brain, he swore. 'Another pair of jeans ruined.'

His erection freed, he pushed into her. After a moment or hour, he couldn't be sure. Her transformation was nearly complete, she squirmed around. She loved doggy style.

His hands clung to the fur on her flanks, felt the silky smoothness, felt the muscles ripple beneath the fur. The rain dampened her fur, heightening the scent of her musk. It reached his nostrils and exploded in his brain. He rammed past her tail as his transformation began.

Imagine holding your breath for a month. That's what it's like for the demon stuffed inside Glen. The chance to finally take a deep lungful is an indescribable release. The sensation was like bursting through the surface of a cold, dark lake, and climaxing. Glen loved when he could time his own climax with the release of his demon. The combination would explode in him. A molten hot flash that flared through his body, through his brain as his human side faded away. He threw his head back, his spine creaked, and his face peeled open.

Christine's lips quivered, curled back, revealing long white canines. When his claws bite into her flanks, a snarl slid past her fangs, low dipped in dark syrup. He howled in response, his transformation nearly complete.

A small sound, a twig snapped behind Glen. He leaped up, still partially a man, but the demon was in control of the teeth and the fangs. His arm lashed out in a wide swinging arch.

The man that stood looking at Glen had a shocked look in his eyes. Glen's casual swipe had torn the lower part of his face off, casting the jaw and tongue into the field, spewing blood in a broad arch across the young crop.

He stood, eyes wide, his hands came up to touch where his jaw once was, swayed and crumpled to the ground, arms and legs vibrating convulsively, then the skin split, tearing down his face and chest revealing tufts of matted, blood-soaked fur.

Christine padded forward and sniffed the man as the convulsions stilled. A growl rumbled in her throat. She turned to Glen, now full wolf. Softly, they touched noses. He growled back, turned, and together loped across the field, the scent of a herd of elk in their nostrils.

Four hours later, the two grey wolves came walking back, slow, and easy. Christine stumbled first. Her long legs buckled, she fell, bumping into Glen's flank before crashing to the ground. She rolled onto her side, her fur parted, splitting down her back as it had been held together with Velcro. The hair and skin sloughed off her and fell to the ground like ash from a fire. The ripping sound mixed with her whimpering as it turned to a cry. She stood as perfect as the day she was born. Every cut and bruise healed. Glen extended his snout, sniffed once, then he too began the painful return. After a few minutes, Glen stood and took Christine's hand. Together they walked back smiling, holding hands, naked and satisfied. The rain had stopped, leaving the field muddy and rich with smells.

"Shit." Christine said, "I guess we'll have to do something about him." She stood looking at the half-man that lay on a ground darkly stained with blood.

"He's one of us. I thought your dad was the first."

"Shit, I don't know. I don't know. I never really knew my dad. I only found out what he was after he turned me, and he was gone by then."

"I thought he went to the Judge and all that?"

"Ya, I found that out from Jacob."

"Jacob?"

"Ya, an old friend of my dad's. He found me after I had changed the first time. Nearly bit off his head, but he's a tough fucker." She smiled, "He's got a deal too."

"Does everyone from your hometown have a deal?"

"No…" She looked at him with a withering eye roll, "but there are a lot."

"Do you recognize this guy? Is he from around Accord?" Glen crouched down, looking at the man's face.

"Naw, can't be." She stood, hands on her hips, looking out at the fields. "No, he's definitely not from back home. He's wearing a suit fer fuck sake." Glen watched her every movement, mesmerised. Her nakedness, the stuff of his dreams ever since they met. The fact that just below her flawless skin was a demon of hair and fangs made her even more exciting to him.

Noticing, she looked down at him and smiled, completely aware of her power over him.

"So, what do you think we should do with him?" She turned away from a distance. "And his car."

The car had been parked down the road from where they had turned off. It was a nondescript grey rental.

"Was that the car following us?"

Glen stood and walked to a point where he could see the car.

"Ya, I think so. it's hard to tell." he frowned. "What in hell did he want?"

Christine bent and lifted the body onto her shoulder. Glen watched her, enjoying the power in her slight frame. He glanced at the spot where the body had lain, looking for anything left behind. Other than the bloodstain, there was nothing. Christine walked toward the car, the man's arms dangling past her butt.

The sun was not up yet, but the sky was lightning in the east.

"We should hurry. The sun'll be up soon."

"Ya, I know. Well, you could help."

Glen ran a couple of steps to get in front of Christine as she reached the parked car. He reached over her shoulder and dug into the man's pocket till he found the keys. After a few moments of fumbling, he unlocked the trunk. Christine dumped the body into the open trunk. She stood back and looked down at the man. Her shoulder was smeared with blood. Glen slid his hand down her back, smearing the blood till his hand cupped her butt, covering it with blood. It aroused him, and he pulled her close.

"Stop that! We ain't got time for that right now, member?'

He sighed and closed the trunk.

"Could your father have gifted him?"

"I don't see how. My dad stayed to hisself, mostly." She turned to look down the road. The sun was just peeking over the horizon, lacing the road with long, thin cobalt shadows.

"What I don't get is why your dad did this to you?"

"Oh, he didn't know he gave me this 'gift'. I'm sure he didn't even know he could. He didn't do it to the Carsons."

"Carsons?"

"Ya, He killed the whole Carson family. He thought Johnny Carson had kidnapped me."

"The comedian?"

"Ha, no, the car dealer. He had a dealership in the city. It's closed now. After the whole family was killed by a 'bear'." She made air quotes. "I don't know why they always say a bear did it."

"Well, aren't bears ferocious beasts?"

"I read somewhere that the most ferocious creature in the northern forest was the wolverine."

"The guy from the movies?"

"God, sometimes you can be so fucking dumb. No, not the movies, not the comics, neither. It's a kinda weasel."

"A weasel couldn't kill a whole family," he said sceptically.

"No? You sure? I hear tell, they are meaner than… well, I don't rightly know, but they are mean."

"We better get this car out of here."

"Ya, I have been thinking bout that. Member Billie?"

Glen glanced at Christine, trying not to notice her nakedness. "No, I don't think so."

"Ya s'pose not. He's gone now. He was marked too." She paused, then looked at Glen, "Anyway, his folk had a farm not far from here. It's abandoned. Nobody's gonna find the car there, at least not for a while."

"K, that sounds good."

Christine turned and climbed into the car.

"Don't you want to put some clothes on?"

She started the car, rolled down the window, and grinned a wicked smile. "Just follow me."

She stomped on the gas pedal. Glen leaped back as the car tore away from him, spitting gravel.

Glen ran back to the Jeep and jumped in. By the time he got turned around and back on the road, all he could see was her dust cloud. He raced after her.

He was starting to catch up when she vanished. He kept roaring on, hoping to see her up ahead. When he didn't, he let up on the gas, slowed, then he saw the tracks in the grass-covered approach. Tall grass and young saplings filled the overgrown yard, its boundary marked by thick mature trees planted years ago when the farm was still in use to make a windbreak. The trees had grown heavy and thick, laced with scrub and weeds. Hidden in the trees, weathered grey buildings stood partially revealed in the new morning sun.

Deeper into the yard stood an old, weathered house, its back broken. The roof sagged in the middle. The first step on returning to the ground.

Glen climbed out of the Jeep. The tracks in the deep grass from the rental car went through the yard, past the house, then turned and entered a grey barn. Its large doors stood open, revealing a shadowed interior. After a minute from the shadows, Christine stepped into the sunlight.

The sight of her, golden in the deep grass with dust floating about her, took Glen's breath away. He stopped and stared at her, slack jawed. She looked at him.

"Well? Are you going to help me, or what?"

When he didn't answer, she laughed. "Come on, help me close the door."

He shook his head and walked forward, wading through the thigh-high grass to help push the drooping doors shut.

The doors had rotted to a point most of the screws holding the hinges had fallen out. Glen grabbed the door and shoved it more or less in place.

"Is that as far in as the car will go?" Glen asked.

Christine gave him a withering look. "Yes. What do you think?"

"Ok, ok." he shoved the door up and forward. It ended up leaning forward against the trunk of the car. "That will have to do."

"No one will find it here. Nobody comes here ever. You bring my clothes?"

"I… I… You left in such a hurry. I…" he grimaced, "you're fucking with me."

She laughed. "Yup. We got fresh clothes in the Jeep, member silly?" She kissed him, took his hand, and they walked to the Jeep, hand in hand. As Christine pulled on her jeans, Glen removed the top panels from the Jeep and stowed them in the back. Christine climbed into the Jeep, leaned the seat all the way back and stretched out. She purred.

Glen climbed in and started the Jeep. He backed up as Christine sat forward, slipped her t-shirt over her head, and reclined with a grin. "Going to go topless in the topless Jeep." Glen grinned back as they pulled out of the abandoned yard and eased onto the gravel road, heading back to the highway that would take them back to the city.

The sound of the Jeep's engine rolled away, followed by a cloud of dust. After a few minutes, the dust settled and quiet returned, the small sounds returned to the grass covered yard. A tiny multitude of furry creatures returned to their tentative scurrying, birds returned to their song, and insects returned to their buzzing. Even the light wind in the tops of the trees seemed louder, more present, as if freed to breathe after the intrusion.

The yard had remained silent and untouched for many years. After the old lady, the last of the family had passed, the house and the outbuildings sat, only the memories and ghosts to wander the small rooms. The wood siding was rotted, the roof leaked as the inevitable slow-motion collapse trudged forward. Each day had slid past, stacked onto the next unchanging, and unnoticed, only the changing seasons marking time. The creatures of the yard would have expected that this single invasion was an anomaly. Not one of their tiny brains could have imagined it could happen again, and so soon.

The afternoon sun touched the tops of the trees, shifting to gold when the first foreign sound crossed the grass. The creatures as one froze, fell silent, bellies tight to the ground, all senses tense and alert. Small noses twitched, ears flitted, searching for the noise that signalled danger.

It had come from the shed at the far side of the open grassy yard. A low, slow scratching sound that edged upward towards a low screech. The sound came again, louder, and insistent, until it became frantic.

It stopped. When it started again, it was deeper, more deliberate. Then, with an explosion of tearing sheet metal and splintering wood, the barn door canted sideways before falling to the grass. A second later, a massive brown and grey wolf stepped slowly down from the trunk of the car and walked out into the yard. Lifting its nose high in the air, it sniffed, turning its head back and forth, searching.

With a slow growl, it lowered its head and with a long loping stride it ran across the yard, leaping from the gravel road and trotted out into the field. Its snout tasted the air until it found what it was searching for, then it ran, covering ground with remarkable speed.

Christine lay on her back in the passenger seat humming to herself, watching the morning sky through the open roof of the Jeep. A dark streak of a bird or soft white cloud occasionally broke the blue. Further up, nearly invisible, a shape of a high-flying bird. A lighter shade of blue against the sky colour. She smiled, enjoying the warm breeze on her bare skin.

In minutes, she was asleep. Glen watched her drift from enjoying the drive, the music, and the air to sleep as he knew she would. She always fell almost straight to sleep after a run.

Inside, he felt the strength of his feelings for her. They had come over him so fast, so powerfully, he had been staggered. She had exploded his life. In the back of his mind, he knew it was partly to do with the wolf in him. Partly a pack thing, but he felt so lucky to have her, to be part of this. It felt as though he had won the lottery. It had just landed in his lap.

He continued to glance from the road to her. He watched her slip into a deeper sleep. She pulled her legs in, rolled onto her side, and curled into a small ball. No longer his sexy girlfriend.

Reaching behind to the back seat, he grabbed his jacket, pulled it forward and covered her, tucking the coat around her. He slowed, feeling no need to rush. He leaned back and watched the landscape pass.

It wasn't long before Glen found his own eyes drifting down. He grunted as his head snapped up and his body jerked. He looked around, blinking, realising he had been asleep for minutes. He laughed lightly, then glanced at Christine, still sound asleep.

A minute later, he found what he was looking for, up ahead, a small approach that led from the highway. He slowed, pulled onto the shoulder. A truck roared past, horn blaring.

The gravel road he turned onto stretched out dead straight ahead. He followed it for a few minutes, then pulled off, parking behind a small stand of poplar trees. He shut the Jeep off, ratcheted his seat back, looked up at the clear blue sky through the open roof, and was asleep in a second.

When he woke, he woke confused. He had been deep asleep and had had no dreams. He wasn't sure where he was. All he knew was he was in his Jeep. But why, he could not remember.

Christine was asleep facing him. Her eyes raced behind her lids, frantic like a trapped bird.

He rocked the seat up and stared through the windshield at a tall naked man standing in the gloaming, looking back at him.

He was tall and very thin. An older man, grey in his unkempt hair. Grey hair on his chest, stomach, and grey stubble on his malformed chin.

With a snap, Glen's mind cleared, he recognized the man who had followed them from the city, whose chin he had ripped off and who they had placed in the trunk of the rental car.

With his right hand, he slowly reached over and touched Christine's shoulder. She made a small noise, sitting bolt upright. Her fingers digging deep into the upholstery, already shifting.

Glen looked back to the man, no longer completely a man. He leaped onto the hood of the Jeep, reached through the open top and tore her fur covered body from the Jeep. Her seat belt snapping. She stared as Glen reached for her.

Glen leaped from the Jeep, landing on all fours fully shifted, lips pulled back from his white k9s. Christine was crouched to his right, her tail whipping. Her hackles were up and there was a deep gash on her shoulder. She didn't seem to notice.

The man was still more human than wolf, and he was smiling. His chin had regenerated mostly covered with thick grey hair, as was his head, shoulders and back. His long arms ended with savage clawed hands hanging loose at his sides. Blood dripped from the talons.

Glen felt her before he saw Christine's leap. She bunched her long, powerful hindquarters and sprung. Glen followed a fraction of a second later. He was in midair when something huge and solid crashed into the side of his head. It spun him sideways, sending him sprawling into the dirt.

He staggered to his feet. Christine was rising unsteadily from the ground in front of the man. He still hadn't shifted. He stood over her, tall and powerful, a slight crouch in his stance but he did not move toward her. Glen shook his head and stepped forward menacingly. A growl was low in his throat.

The man smiled at Glen raising his arm, "Wait," the man said.

Glen paused, surprised. He watched Christine. Her shoulder was now bleeding profusely. She looked dazed.

Glen looked back at the man. He was more human, not completely, but closer. He was smiling.

"We do not have to fight, little one. I knew your father." He said to Christine, "He was in a way my father too."

Christine was slipping into her human shape. A look of confusion in her eyes.

Her first words were more growls than words, "… don't understand. Who are you?"

The man's smile flickered, then returned. "I farmed down the road from him when he was a kid. I knew his father. Not a nice man." He looked down at the ground. "Your father visited my farm one late night. Killed a couple of pigs. I heard the squealing and come out. I thought it were a coyote. I brung my shotgun." He chuckled, "that weren't much help." He laughed again. It was a bitter laugh without any humour.

Christine was standing, holding her right arm. Blood was running down and dripping from her fingers. She looked in pain. She should be healing, but she wasn't.

Glen stepped closer, still fully wolf.

"Yes, he gave me this gift, and I had to figure it out on my own. I'm glad I lived alone." The man looked up at Christine, then past her to the darkening fields. He seemed lost in memory. "When I woke in the barn, I couldn't figure out what had happened. I thought I was dead. I mean a big fucking wolf gad torn ne ya bits, but there I was, naked as the day I was born." He looked at Glen, "Simmer down, son. I mean, I came all this way ya tell you my story. Lest ya could do after killing me, locking in the truck on my rental and leaving me is hear it."

Glen's hackles settled some, suddenly feeling guilty.

The man laughed. "At first it was fun. I loved running through the night hunting. It was so free, but then I found out about the payment."

He looked at Christine pale and naked, "Ain't you just the prettiest little thing." His eyes slid across her body, oily and slow. "You don't know bout the payment, do ya?"

Christine just looked at him, glanced quickly at Glen, then back to the man.

"Payment?"

"Ya, that's what I thought. They told me you weren't told. They shoulda but they didn't. That's the problem with the

Devil and his deals. They always come with strings attached and some ah those strings have nooses." He grinned at his little joke.

"Fucker, you better start talking sense." Christine's voice was tense. Glen recognized the stance. She was losing patience. It wouldn't be too long before she lost it and tore him apart no matter how strong he was.

The man smiled down at her, "Sure, sure little lady. Sure sure. Ya see, you got to pay to play."

"Play? What the fuck are you talking about?"

The man looked at her for a long time, his smile slowly faded leaving behind a cruel hard face. "You can't have this power without paying." He said with a quiet voice.

"This power?"

"Yes, this power. This gift. The change." The man's smile broadened. "The fun wolf thing, little one. The wolf thing." His voice was condescending. Glen groaned.

"You are so young and so naïve. Do you really think there was no payment required? After all this time, did you not feel something was waiting for you?"

Christine said nothing.

"The arrogance of the young. Well, that time has come whether you thunk it were coming or not." He paused and looked out across the field, "You will have to come with me."

"I'm not going nowhere, fucker." Christine straightened, proud and defiant. Glen smiled, loving her all the more for her fierceness.

"I really don't understand. This isn't a choice you can say nope to."

"I can say fuck you..."

"No, you really can't. The Judge will have his due. Promises were made, hands were shook. Your father knew when he walked from the crossroads after meeting The Judge. He knew there was a payment. He knew it would come due. If he hadn't swallowed that silver pill, he would have paid. Ha, I suppose he paid anywho."

"Careful Fucker. Watch what you are saying." Christine stepped forward. The first signs of her change starting.

"Careful? The Deal is the Deal! The Deal is all there is. You're part of the deal. Your daddy made it and I made one too. A new one just for me. A little extra time."

"Extra time?" Christine stepped back, uncertain.

"Ya time. Only got so much. Something about a fucking contract. Some fucking 666 clause. It's all bullshit, but I wanted more time so…" He glanced at Glen, "The payment is you. Nothing less. You are the payment." He chuckled, "At least you are my payment."

The last words came out as a growl. He shifted amazingly fast, nearly blurring with the speed of his attack. Glen was startled. He stood frozen for a second. The man shifted only part way to wolf. His massive clawed hand swung a giant arch through Christine. She seemed to explode.

Glen leaped, his scream of terror and pain cracked, became a feral howl. His talons tore through the terrible red, reaching for the form he could barely make out. He missed. He landed, rolled, claws digging into the ground. His lips pulled back, fangs bared, ready to claw and rip but what he saw stopped his attack.

Through the red he was sure Christine was gone, but there she stood, fur matted with blood, her arm limp at her side, but there was fire in her eyes. Fire and defiance, she was mostly wolf. Her chest heaved. She was in pain, ready to rip and tear. Her eyes softened when she looked at Glen, then she refocused on the man in front of her and leaped. Glen leaped a millisecond after her, a snarl tearing from his lips. From out of nowhere, a blow stunned Glen, throwing him sideways. He tumbled into the dirt. He righted himself, ready to attack, but what he saw stopped him.

The man stood, a tall, lean beast of a man. The muscles on his right arm stood out, stark and hard. He was holding Christine by the throat. She hung limp from the man's clawed hand. She had shifted completely. Her fur was wet and stained. Gouts of gore dripped wetly onto the ground beneath her.

The man shook her like a rag doll, a smile on his face. A smile that did not touch his black eyes.

With a growl, half in pain, half in fury, Glen bunched his hind quarters and leaped, claws and talons outstretched.

The man tossed the tiny body of Christine into Glen's snarling face. It knocked him backward and sideways.

Glen hugged the still body as he crashed to the ground. He held her laying on his side as he shifted back, stroking her fur. His pale, naked body clung to her.

Behind him, he heard the man approach.

"You should have left her alone. She wasn't for you." The man said, his voice, low and rough.

Glen turned his head to look up at him.

"She was mine. I loved her." Glen whispered.

"She was never yours." The man stepped closer. "She was meant for another." He stepped closer still. "She was promised a long time ago to another."

"Promised? What are you talking about?"

"A deal was made. Payment is required."

The man, now right beside Glen, knelt and touched the lifeless body in Glen's trembling arms. She shifted, fur falling away, revealing her perfect, smooth skin. Glen clung to her, his tears falling on her cheeks.

"It is done. Payment had been made."

Glen felt the change. Christine's body changed. Just a small fraction, but he felt it. She shrank a minute amount. Glen held her tighter, then he was holding nothing. Christine fell apart turning into soft grey ashes that crumpled, blown away into the evening air. She drifted through his arms and was gone.

Ashes clung to Glen's damp cheeks and stung his eyes. His tears stopped as he painfully pushed himself up from the ground. He stood looking down at his empty hands. Empty now as his heart. It did not break, it solidified, becoming stone, grey and colourless. Looking down at his empty hands, he watched the claws slide easily from his fingertips.

He spun, snarling, and frozen. The man stood still, a look of abject horror on his face.

"They lied." He said. A look crossed his face. Like a small boy on his birthday who discovered that the fancy wrapped gift is only socks. A mix of incredulity and disappointment. He looked at Glen as his body burst into a ball of flame. Glen stepped back from the sudden heat. The air filled with the smell of a barbeque. The man took a step forward, his arms moving in slow circles as if he were searching for something in the dark. He fell to his knees, then tipped forward, face down on the ground. Like a dying campfire, he crumpled into embers. A slight breeze caught a few of those and tossed them into the night air. Black ash rolled out onto the ground, and he was gone.

Glen stood for a long time in the dark. He turned to watch the morning when he noticed a slight glow to the east. He couldn't think of what he should do now. He was alone with his grief. He had no one to share it with.

He hadn't noticed as he shifted to his human shape. Remembering his neighbour's small fluff ball of a dog allowed the barest minute to shit, only to be dragged home at the end of an angry leash. He felt like that. No choice, just obey the jerk of his leash. He felt a bitter, angry mix of sadness and loss.

With a snarl, he shifted to his wolf and started to run. He ran north with no actual plan, just a desperate need to be where there were no people. He ran chased by his broken heart.

"You can't have the guitar."

7

I HATE THE BLUES

Disco is where it's at. At least, that's what Nathan thought when he was younger. It was the music of his becoming. It played in the background of every significant event in his life. It was playing on the radio when he drank his first beer. It was still on when, after three more, he threw up all over his pal's parent's sofa. It was playing upstairs at a party when in the dark basement, Becky let him undo her bra and feel for the first time those milky firm globes.

Disco filled his life with joy and passion as he danced on roller skates, his skinny leather tie flapping at the Roller rink.

It was playing on the car radio when his dad lost control and slid through an intersection, killing everyone in the car except him. It was there when a girl whose name or face he cannot remember gave him a most awkward gift and took from him his virginity. He said 'took' because he barely knew it was happening. He had been drinking. It was only days after he stood beside his grandma at the funeral of his parents and his little sister. He was numb, barely aware of anything.

He met his wife years later at a KC concert, and they danced their wedding dance to Donna Summer.

Disco was there for every milestone except the one that turned everything in his life upside down.

As disco faded, his life seemed to wash out, to lose colour. Passion seemed to slip away with every breath he took, and nothing he did could recapture it. He and his wife grew increasingly distant until there wasn't any reason to stay together. There were no kids, so it wasn't a big thing. The day he got the notice he was divorced, he cried. He sat in his tiny apartment kitchen and cried like he hadn't since his parents died.

It wasn't his failed marriage. That was just a symptom of the greater loss that he had suffered.

"Well," He said to the darkening kitchen after he had cried himself out, "Now what? What are you going to do? You are a bachelor. Maybe you should go out and find that passion you lost?"

Resolved, he stood, showered, put on some clean clothes, and left his sad excuses for a new start.

It had been years since he had gone out on the town. None of the clubs he had gone to then were around. The few remaining were shadows of their former selves, as sad as the lost, longing individuals that haunted them.

By eleven, he had lost all hope. He was feeling lower than the moment he opened that letter earlier this afternoon. A feeling of loss settled on his shoulders.

He gave up. He just gave up. He decided that he was old and tired, and nothing could save him from his slow, minute-by-minute death. It was inevitable. Like every man before him, he would die hollowed out and alone.

He left the club and started walking back home.

The night was warm and pleasant. As he walked, he dwelled on the mistakes of his life. Running them through, wishing to somehow shift the outcome, feeling the shame and disappointment over and over again. When he looked up, he realised he, out of habit, had been walking to his old home, not his new apartment. He had only moved in a week before. He groaned. He looked down the street toward the home he had shared with his wife. My 'X wife,' he reminded himself. He turned and started trudging back.

He looked for a cab. A few drove past, but none stopped. One even slowed and then sped away as he ran up to it. He swore, shaking his fist, but in reality, he wasn't all that angry, just frustrated and mostly with himself.

The walk took him down several streets he had never walked before, driven sure, but never walked. Finally, he turned into a residential area, walking past some stately homes, mostly dark, but a few had windows lit up and warm.

He paused, looking in the window of a large, beautiful house. Inside, he could see good-looking, happy people standing around, laughing, and smiling.

The night air felt suddenly much colder than it had just a minute before. He felt lonely and clutched by a deep sadness.

He forced himself to move, walking away from the scene that had attracted, captivated, then tortured him.

Once out of the residential area, he came out on the busy street, lit up with small cafes and traffic. It wasn't an area he knew anything about.

He turned in the direction of his apartment. He loped across the street in front of a slow movie streetcar, glanced back at it, then walked backwards, nearly falling over a low fence surrounding a small patio.

The sign over the bright cafe read Ol' Tom's. A sandwich board perched outside proclaimed Ol' Tom's Backroom open stage.

The idea flared in his mind like distant forgotten fireworks. Live music! The room was full of youthful passion. His spirit lifted, and he walked into the cafe with a smile. The front of the cafe was nearly empty. A couple of tables held people leaning in and talking in the shadows. A bartender leaned casually on the bar flirting with a young server.

He walked past and nodded as he followed the noise to the back room.

When he turned the corner, the pure, unfiltered energy staggered him. He paused, blinking at the glow from the empty stage. Everywhere was movement. Faces bright in the stage lights swam in the dark of the room. It was a scene of chaotic energy but underlying it all was a focus, an intent. This energy was directed. It was aimed at a very specific anticipated goal. Under the cacophony of voices was a second layer of sound. A sound of guitar strings being tuned. It added a drone, an underlayer of tone that wrapped the room.

He felt the magic of this night. Somehow, he was meant to be here. This was designed, preordained, a destiny he had to fulfil.

He swelled with power and passion, real passion. He breathed it in, filling his lungs with it. He became a sponge, sucking up the passion, the youth, the energy.

A table to his right had an empty chair. He slipped in and sat, a grin on his face. This is what he wanted. No, this is what he needed. He looked around, catching glimpses of faces, young and filled to the brim with nervous excitement. 'The Dream' shone in each and every glassy-eyed hopeful with a rhyme and three chords.

Absently, he ordered a beer from the pretty server that had been with the bartender when he entered. When it arrived, he reached for it out of habit. The taste, coolness, and carbonation were so profound that they described a beer's very essence. He stared at the glass, looking at the amber liquid, marvelling at the depth and honesty of the experience. It was just a pint of beer, but in this moment, it was the experience of every beer he had ever tasted.

At some point, he could never tell when exactly everything had changed. A shift in the air, it slowed, dipped in syrup, viscous thick, as golden as fresh honey, as fresh as a butter commercial. And in that split second, in the fraction of time that stretched in the future, lost in the infinite, somewhere in that universe of time. He saw the world as it was, behind the curtain that had been pulled over his eyes and thickened as the years piled up, turning into a milky film that clouded his every moment and hid his true self from him. Then, with that cleared and pulled from his vision, he saw what he had lost, saw the being of light and shadow he was. A person he used to know and knew well. A human he had revelled in being.

He ignored the tear that slid quietly down his cheek and tried very hard not to notice the loss that swept through him. He knew that all these years, what he missed, like an amputated limb, was hidden from him, not really lost but waiting, just inches from his fingertips but miles from his reach. It was the reason. The reason people fight to survive, the reason people, against all odds, fight to stay alive, search for love, and write words on a page that no one will ever read or hear sung.

The reason every single person here had spent hours learning to play their guitar was to write down those private words that described the moments of real truths that had once touched their worlds. It was the impetus of the dream, the sharing, the very human need to communicate. It bound every person in the room. He looked at every face he could see and felt a kinship that transcended anything he had ever known before. He loved them all. They were, at that moment, his family, bonded by their very humanity.

The door that slammed down on him took his breath and left him gasping. Its black weight shut him off from the room with a finality, leaving him cold, shivering and alone.

He looked around the room, trying to find the cause. He saw everyone looking around as well, aware of the change. He watched as a man walked in and leaned against the back wall. A tight thin smile on his lips. He was tall and disturbingly thin, dressed in a suit. When he saw the dog, he gasped. The sight was so out of place, so foreign, it shocked him. He watched as the dog sat calmly beside his master, surveying the room with pale, almost white eyes.

There was an amplified screech and a pop as someone walked on the empty stage and plugged in.

Nathan turned from the odd sight, wondering when the last time he had seen a dog in a bar. Somewhere deep inside of him, his inner voice cried a warning that he didn't heed.

The man on stage looked as though he had been living rough for some time. Even his black guitar was beaten and scarred.

Nathan wasn't a guitar player and actually never had any musical inclinations. Still, with its deep gashes and cracked black paint, this instrument attracted him like no object had ever before. A part of him wanted to touch the surface, to caress it. He wanted to possess it, to make it his own. He was shocked at how powerful the feeling was. He leaned forward, forgetting his beer, forgetting the people around him, forgetting why he had entered the club, even forgetting himself, lost in his single-minded focus on the guitar that the strange man on stage held.

Then the man on stage strummed a cord, and the spell was broken, replaced by another equally as powerful. Nathan sat back in his seat, mesmerised. Around him, people quieted and stilled. By the time the first song was finished, the entire room was silent. No one spoke, no one moved. The entire restaurant was utterly and wholly fixed on the man on stage.

The second song began. It rang through the club, dripping with anger and violence. Nathan's chest tightened as the emotion wrapped around him. A gasp escaped past his lips, joined by the rest of the audience as each person in the room felt the power of the song wash through, like a physical wave cresting through the room, touching each upturned face.

Nathan watched the man on stage scream into the mic. Flakes of dust, gold and red in the stage lights floated from the strings as each chord was played. Like the sparks from a campfire, they filled the air, radiating out from the stage to be breathed in by the audience.

Nathan felt the particles as they entered his lungs. Tiny sparks filled him with a radiance he hadn't felt since he was 12. His body tensed, joints creaking with the tension. His spine arched. His fingers bent as they gripped the table, squeaking on the wood. He breathed deep, sucking in as much as he could. His throat burned as a heat filled his chest. Around him, people began to weep with deep, heaving sobs. Nathan glowed, mouth open, eyes closed. He was filled with a power.

He bent forward, head nearly touching the table, then sensing eyes on him, he looked around until his eyes locked onto the strange eyes of the dog. For an uncomfortable moment, they stared at each other. Nathan's unease grew until he couldn't take it anymore. He looked away inexplicably, feeling shame. He looked at the floor in front of the dog. The shadows cast from the stage light writhed viper-like. Finally, he looked back at the stage. The ragged man was now playing a different song. He had missed the end of the last song. He realised he didn't know how many songs the man had played. There was a two-song limit, but he had been on stage for much longer than that.

The song he was playing was a sad, torturous composition. He felt the pain slide over him, a blanket of sadness.

A girl screamed in terror, breaking the spell. He tore his eyes from the stage to the screaming girl. Her eyes were wide, the whites blazed in the dark. She was staring past the audience to the back of the room.

Nathan turned in his chair to see what had terrified her. It was the man who had come in with the dog, but he was no longer a man. He was something other, something altogether horrific and monstrous. Nathan stood slowly, staring at the creature, unable to look away. Around him, the audience continued to watch the stage, listening to the man who played on.

But then it all shifted. The man at the back of the room smiled at Nathan, who smiled back. Golden dust motes floated around him, and a sense of contented well-being engulfed him. He sat lost once again in the music.

This song was different. It reached into Nathan to a place he didn't know existed, a place that lay near a spot disco had touched. In the rhythm and lyrics of the song, he recognized a feeling. It drew on him, pulling at his soul, tugging out a desire he didn't know he had ever wanted; now, it became overpowering. He heard echoes of another instrument, one he felt inside him, a texture, a shape he could touch in his hands.

He didn't know what it was exactly, but he had to find it.

When the song ended, he felt a staggering loss, almost a death. The man on stage sat still, calmly looking out at the audience. Then, as if a decision had been made, he dropped the guitar as he stood. It slipped from his lap and shattered as if it had been made of glass. Nathan watched, numb, as the man left the stage, unsure of what he was supposed to do now, unsure of where he was supposed to go. He knew he had to do something urgently. He sat frozen, needing movement but wholly lost at what that meant. A thing had woken inside him, a thing that demanded attention. He just didn't know what it was. Finally, the audience stirred around him. He rose and left the club with the other members of the audience, wandering aimlessly into the chill night air. A newly formed passion, a desperate need coursing through him.

It was becoming light when Nathan found himself standing in front of his home. The grey light washed the colour from the well-kept brick house where he no longer lived. As he watched, a light came on in the kitchen. He watched his ex-wife walk slowly past the window. She would be going to make coffee, and with a morning as nice as this one, she would be going to sit in the garden.

Nathan turned his back on the scene, on a life that had ended, and walked away. He knew somewhere deep down he should feel sad, or even angry, something, but he felt nothing. Just a sense that there was an empty space, a hollow that this woman or the life she represented. The hollow was something else, something new.

In the afternoon, when he woke in his apartment lying face down on his scratchy couch, he could not remember what had happened the night before. Something had happened; he was sure of it, but the more he thought about it, the fuzzier his memory seemed to get. Then the headaches started. At first, it was a pressure, as if a spike was bearing down on his skull.

After a few days, the pain moved behind the back of his eyes. There it stayed, hovering, claws out, ready to tear into him.

Every time he thought of that night, trying to piece together what he had done, what he had experienced, the pain made him squint, tears welling up and running down his cheeks.

For several weeks, it got increasingly worse until it was a constant low constant ache. It kept him awake at night, and when he did finally get to sleep, it was fraught with nightmares. Laced with dark, ambiguous shapes that loomed just out of sight.

In his apartment on a sunny Saturday with the curtains drawn tight against the light, he sat in the darkest room and sipped water, a half-empty bottle of painkillers on the floor beside him. He had taken to popping painkillers like candy. He swallowed another pill, hoping to stave off the oncoming headache he could feel building, a growing wave of pain he feared would overwhelm him.

But the headache shifted. The pain paused just over the horizon of his mind. He heard quietly at first, a melody, just a hint of a song, but as he listened, it grew, built into music so beautiful, so enticing, he could feel it somewhere deep inside him. Note by note, line by line, the threads wrapped themselves around him. A giant hug that dispelled the pain and the doubt, leaving him revitalised and at peace.

He leaned back against the wall, eyes closed, and let the energy wash over him like waves that had rolled in from far out at sea. Waves that whispered stories of exotic lands seeped in dark magics. He felt the power. Felt the echo, a reflection of his own heartbeat.

For the first time in weeks, he felt calm inside. There was no headache waiting to cripple him. No disabling pain coming to tear at him any second. He felt like a great weight lifted from him, a swallow of cool, clean water, a deep lung full of fresh air. He breathed in great gulps of air and relaxed.

The memories of the night in Ol' Tom's Backroom exploded in his brain. He leaped to his feet, his brain whirling with emotions. All the feelings he had experienced that incredible night came rushing in, overwhelming him. He staggered, bracing himself against the wall. JOY! Pure joy filled him as he remembered the music. His body spasmed, and he fell back to the floor.

That music that he had heard and felt coming from that man on stage, from that dark guitar, was all he wanted. No, not wanted, needed.

He rose on unsteady feet with a single thought in his head. "Find that man and his guitar."

***

The bar he walked into was like so many had stepped into, full of hope this would be the one. It had been years and hundreds, perhaps thousands of bars, and always there was the scent of what he sought, but not the real thing. He was, he knew, an addict, but his addiction was of something so rare he had only found it the single time. That had been enough for him to wander following rumours, stories told to him by drunken men who may or not be full of shit. His bullshit metre had gotten pretty good.

He had gone through his savings within the first few months. Now he worked odd jobs and the occasional freelance consulting job he got from his one remaining friend, although the last gig was several months ago, so maybe that friend had grown tired of his obsession like all the rest.

He also knew he looked rough. He was skinny. His clothes draped off his bones. They were clean but worn. His face was sunken and deeply lined. His long, dark beard and hair were peppered liberally with grey.

He walked up to the bar where a woman was pulling a pint for a couple of farmers. They sat leaning forward on their elbows, watching the amber liquid fill the glance with anticipation on their weathered faces. He watched as each reached forward as the bartender placed the glasses in front of them.

"What kin I get ya, hun?"

The woman had moved quickly up to him with a careful smile.

"Is there live music tonight?" He said, sliding onto a stool two down from the farmers.

"Yes, every Wednesday and Saturday. Thursday is wing night."

"Do you know who's playing?" He asked.

"No, hun. Some new guy I ain't heard a'fore. You wanna beer?"

"Ya...ya, that would be great. Thanks."

She stepped to the taps and pulled him a pint. She placed a coaster with the devil's face on it and placed the dripping pint in front of him.

"Thanks." He reached for it, his mouth already tasting the cold beer.

"You want ta run a tab?"

He paused, smiled, and pulled a twenty from his jeans pocket. "No. I'll pay as I go. Thanks."

"Ok, hun." She swapped the bill for his change and moved down the bar to pull some fresh pints for the two farmers.

The beer tasted good, really good. Maybe the best-tasting beer he had had since that life-changing beer he drank the night he found his addiction. He smiled a tired smile at the memory. Slipping from the stool, he walked deeper into the half-full bar. To his right, past the high-top tables, was a pool table with a group of bikers noisily laughing and playing.

Past the end of the wooden bar, the room opened up, revealing a large space with a small, dark stage.

Nathan pulled out a chair and sat at a table against the wall.

He was halfway through his beer when the stage lighting came on and the room lights dimmed.

A man walked in, looking at a paper. He had long dark hair parted in the middle that he probably had since he was a teen. Now it was at odds with his expanding bald spot and belly.

The man glanced at Nathan as he sat to the right of the stage. On a small table, he had a soundboard and a mic. He would be the MC for the evening. Nathan had seen similar setups a few hundred times.

As if drawn by the stage light, people started wandering, some from other parts of the bar, drinks in hand. Others came in from outside and sat looking around for a server to get their first and most important drink.

Nathan finished his pint and was surprised to find the waitress that had served him when he came in standing beside him, smiling.

"Can I getcha another, hun?"

"Umm. Ya, that would be great, thank you."

His empty glass was whizzed away, and sooner than he thought possible, another replaced it.

He dug into his jeans and pulled out a pair of fives.

"Keep the change." He said.

"Thanks, hun." She smiled and moved to the next table.

Nathan took a swallow of his fresh beer when from the stage sound system screamed a piercing demon cry that scared Nathan. He flinched, almost spilling his beer. He placed the glass down on the table and looked up to the stage.

The man that walked toward the stage was bent and old, with a shrivelled, dry look to him. His worn clothes hung from his thin frame, and he moved as though each step cost him.

Most singers walked to the stage with frenetic energy, part fear, part anticipation. He stepped up on stage with none of that. He sat almost as though he were resigned to it, as though he had no choice in the matter. He held a guitar. Its surface was nearly black with deep scars, scars that were nearly gouged through the wood.

Nathan glanced around the room. The tables were filling, but no one seemed to be watching the stage.

The first chord changed that. The man seated in the light attacked the guitar. Beating the strings with a fierceness that bordered on violence. Most players displayed reverence for their instrument. This man showed only contempt and anger. He slammed his fingers past the strings, up, then down. Shifting from one pained-filled chord to the next.

Then he closed his eyes and began to sing. The words ripped from his throat, dripping with anger and pain.

Nathan was enthralled. Here was the power he had sought all these years.

He gripped his forgotten pint until his knuckles cracked and the glass threatened to shatter. He leaned forward across his table, intent on the man on stage.

Then, after two songs, the man on stage stopped, rose, and walked off the stage.

Nathan sat stunned. He had expected thirteen songs. He had expected the life-altering experience he had had all those years ago. For several seconds he sat his mouth agape, unsure of what just happened. He slowly realised that another player was stepping up. With a shake of his head, he looked around the bar.

He couldn't find the man with the guitar. Nathan stood; his table forgotten. It tipped forward, rocking. His half-finished beer tipped, spilling across the table. He didn't notice. His eyes raked the crowd, looking for the guitarist. On his third sweep of the bar, he saw the man's hat at the door just leaving the bar.

Nathan shoved his way through the now-crowded bar. He did not notice the curses of the people he shoved out of his way.

He burst from the bar into the pink neon night, but the guitarist he pursued was gone. Nathan ran down the five steps and out into the gravel parking lot, looking wildly about.

The man was nowhere to be seen. Like the bar, the parking lot was now jammed with trucks of various descriptions. Nathan walked around the lot, increasingly despondent. After years of searching to be so close and losing him now was too much.

At the dark edge of the lot farthest from the buzzing neon, Nathan sat on one of the Timbers driven into the ground that marked the edge of the lot. He looked into the night. It was nearly a full moon wreathed with purplish clouds.

"Now what?" He asked the night.

"Who are you?" The man's voice was quiet, but the sound of it startled Nathan. He leaped back a pace. "What do you want with me?" The old man stood just outside the pool of light cast by the parking lot's overhead light. Nathan could barely see him. Just glints off the light off his buttons and a flash off the guitar case's latches.

Nathan wasn't sure what to say. He had waited years to be here in this spot, talking to this man. He had rehearsed what he would say many times, but now he couldn't think. He stepped forward, palms up, "I just wanted…"

The old man moved with surprising quickness and punched Nathan in the nose. Instantly, his eyes filled with tears. He staggered back, tripping and falling heavily to the ground on his butt, legs straight out. He blinked, unbelieving. John stepped into the light, extending his hand to help Nathan stand.

"I had to make sure you wasn't one of them."

"Wasn't one of who?"

Nathan took John's hand and stood, rubbing his face. No blood, but he was going to have a black eye. All his nerves were gone. Now he was just annoyed. "Why'd ya hit me? I just wanted to ask you a question."

"Well, you ain't one of them, so what's yer question?"

Nathan thought for a second, "I was there… that night when you played your thirteen songs…"

"Ah. So that's what this is all about. Look, kid. I don't got what yer looking for. And I only played one of my songs."

"So, I was right. The others were the devil's. How'd you find him? How'd he give the songs? We're there anymore. Do you still know them? Do you still play them? Were they hard to learn? How long did it take you? Can you teach me?"

With a deep sigh, John held up a weary hand. "You fuckers. You have tormented me ever since that night. None of you realise what I did for you. What I sacrificed." John's voice edged upward, his anger tightening his throat, "You don't get it. Those songs were not a gift. They were a trap. A way for him to capture you all. Instead, all he got was me. You want those songs because they were designed to snare you. Make you dream about them. They aren't the answer. They are the end. End of everything. I mean everything!" John screamed the last words, leaning in, his nose inches from Nathan's face. Nathan braced, expecting to be punched again, but John seemed to deflate the anger and the fire, leaving him as quickly as it had flared.

"I wish I had known then. I wish I understood what I was giving up. What I was going to lose." He looked down at the guitar case in his hand. He lifted it into the air, "All for this…" he shook it, "for this accursed hunk of wood."

Nathan looked at the case, not understanding.

"But the songs. You got that sound, man! It's so real, so honest. It's worth anything!" Nathan almost pleaded.

John looked at him, a resigned sadness in his eyes. He knew he could not convince this man of his truth, and in truth, he was too tired to try. He had had this very same conversation so many times over the years. He had always failed to change that manic look in their eyes. Many of the people he had tried so hard to save had sought him out, trying to capture what they had only glimpsed that terrible night.

John turned from Nathan and began to step back into the dark.

"Wait! Where are you going? I need your help! You can't leave. I've searched for you for years."

John turned. "What do you think I can do for you?"

"Tell me the secret! Tell me how I can have the sound."

"You want the sound?"

"Yes! More than anything in the world. I need it!"

John looked at this intense man.

"Ok." He said quietly. He stood half in shadow and stared at the man. He looked into the night, testing the decision that had just touched his mind.

"Here." Looking Nathan straight in the eyes, John held out his guitar case. "It's yours." His voice was quiet, almost a whisper.

"Really?" Nathan hesitated, then reached eagerly for his prize.

The moment his fingers touched the handle, the moment he took the weight of the case and what lay inside, the night air was suddenly filled with the buzzing of thousands of black flies.

"Oh fuck! They're here!" John screamed as he turned and ran into the dark. Nathan watched him vanish, his free hand waving at the swarm of flies as it dissipated.

"Good evening, Sir." The voice came from right behind Nathan, making him jump. Behind him stood a tall, thin man, a silhouette in the harsh overhead light. His face was completely shadowed, but Nathan could just pick out the man's unsettling, toothy smile.

"I must congratulate you on your recent acquisition."

"My acquisition?"

"Yes, the fine instrument in your hand."

Nathan looked down at the well-travelled case in his hand. He longed to open the case, to touch what he had so long dreamt of. But, most of all, he needed to know if he did indeed possess the dream that awoke in him all those years ago in Ol' Tom's Backroom.

"Do not worry, Sir. It is Truly yours."

"Wait, who are you?" The question popped into his mind. He was surprised it hadn't occurred to him to ask sooner."

The tall, strange man seemed poised to answer but said, "Ah, here he is."

From the dark, a tall silhouette identical to the man who spoke came walking, accompanying John, his head down, defeated.

"John! So good to finally meet you. I have, of course, heard all about you."

Once again, Nathan was surprised at how fast the older man could move. John leaped forward with a huge haymaker punch aimed at the tall, thin man. Nathan watched as the man disintegrated into a cloud of buzzing flies and then reformed almost immediately.

"Very amusing, John. Very amusing." He said without humour.

On the highway, two funnels of light followed by the snap and growl of a pair of motorbikes gearing down to turned into the parking lot.

Nathan looked across the parking lot to watch them rumble off the highway, through the lot to pull up under the neon near the door of the bar.

When he looked back, a long black car slowly pulled up beside him. The two tall, smiling men watched it approach, their smiles seeming to glow.

John pulled back but was held by the thin man's slender fingers on his shoulders.

The man who stepped out was a picture of poise and ease. He smiled amiably at Nathan as he straightened his tie and walked up to John.

"So, this is the famous John Whitey." He looked around at the smiling man and briefly at Nathan.

"I owe you so much you can't imagine." He said, looking back to John.

John looked back at this new arrival, frowning.

"What the fuck is this? Who are you? You are not Ol' Tom." John said.

"Why I am the Judge." said the man with a flair, as if he was known and should be recognized.

"The Judge? This doesn't make any sense."

"No, suppose it is rather confusing. I don't think this is the time to get into it. Suffice it to say, I am extremely happy to finally meet you." Then, looking around, his eyes landed on the guitar case in Nathan's hand, and that is the guitar?"

Nathan shifted the case slightly away from the Judge protectively.

The Judge smiled. "And you have given freely to Nathan here."

John said nothing.

"Well, that means I need to deal with him. Too bad. I had hoped to deal with you, John, but it's not to be. I can, however, offer you something for all you did. What is it I can give, John? Is there anything you need or want?"

John stared at the Judge. "I'm done. I want my deal to be done. I'm sick of playing in bars to crowds who can't be bothered to listen. I just want to go home."

"Ha, well, absolutely! That is very easily done! Consider your contract done."

"That easy? Contracts do not go away. Not ever."

"Well, yes, that is true, but for you, I will make an exception. It is as if it never happened. You are free!" The Judge smiled and raised his arms wide to indicate the world around him. "Go where you will. In fact, tell my driver, and I will send you there in style." The Judge stepped back and opened the back door of the elegant squat car he had arrived in.

John hesitated, unsure of what was happening. Then, making the decision, he quickly stepped forward and slipped into the waiting car. The Judge, smiling, closed the door. After a second, the car began to roll forward out of the parking lot onto the highway and, in seconds, was gone.

The Judge watched the car drive away, then turned to Nathan.

"You can't imagine how much I owe that man." He paused. "Now let's talk. Your guitar has put you in a rather enviable position."

"You can't have the guitar."

"Oh, my no. I don't want your guitar, nor do I want the sound it carries. No, those are yours. What I want is the case, or rather something in the case."

Nathan frowned. "Ok," was all he could say.

"Splendid. Why don't you put the case right up here on the hood, and we'll complete our business?"

Nathan turned to see the black car, or its identical twin, parked behind him.

"Ummm. Ok." Hefting the case up, he carefully placed it on the hood and snapped open the clasps. Inside was the most beautiful guitar he had ever seen. It was a deep red, nearly black, heavily scarred, just as he recalled it from that night. Reverently, he reached forward with both hands and, from the black lining, pulled his new treasure. It seemed to hum in his hands.

"Ha, it does suit you. I am sure you will do some incredible things with that instrument. Now, may I?" The Judge indicated the case.

"Yes, yes, of course," Nathan said without taking his eyes off his prize.

The Judge stepped forward and touched the case, sliding his hand across the velvet lining to the centre of the case, where pics were stored. He opened the tiny door and drew out a small leather pouch. He smiled as he opened the drawstring and poured the contents into his hand.

Four ancient silver coins spilled out to glint in the harsh overhead light. As quickly as he had spilled them, he returned to the bag, cinched it shut, and slipped it into his pocket.

"Four closer." He whispered then as though remembering where he was; he looked up and smiled broadly.

"I believe that concludes our business." He looked at one of the tall, thin, smiling men. "Yes?"

"Sir, the contract is satisfied."

"Excellent." The Judge clapped his hands together. "It's time. And you, my musical friend, you are free to roam the back roads and, well, whatever you do. Pluck that six-string demon to your heart's content."

Nathan's mouth remained open, still unsure of what had just happened. His hand gripped the neck of his guitar. His dream that he had followed for so many years had only got as far as talking to Whitey. He had never thought of what happened after, after he met, talked to, and convinced John to give him the sound. That's as far as the dream went. Now what? He looked at his prize, looked at The Judge and suddenly, a whole new dream opened like the wings of a new and wonderful dark butterfly.

A COLD HAND

8

MAN OF FLIES

Monday

Phil angrily stared down at his desk, at the pool of light with papers strewn about as if the files, notes pertaining to the cases he was working on, were withholding the solution. The office was empty. He was tired and frustrated. The receptionist had left at 3 to go to a dentist's appointment. Allen had headed home hours ago, or rather he went to his motel room. Like himself, his marriage had fallen apart. This was Allen's second walk through the wringer, and he seemed to take it better than the last time.

Phil was a sizable man, slightly over six feet and heavy. He wore a button collar shirt uncomfortably tucked into jeans. His wife had bought his clothes for him. He had rarely noticed, what he wore was never important to him. Now, of course, she was gone, and his clothes were looking tired and worn.

He leaned back, hands behind his neck, and groaned. He had been sitting for several hours working the case that had come in early that morning. It was a favour for a friend and a former client, so more of an acquaintance, but it was a corporate gig. They usually paid well and were straightforward. But, in the back of Phil's mind, he knew that the case you take on to help a 'friend' is often the one that turns into an onerous nightmare. No good deed goes unpunished.

This case was a two-parter. The first part was to find a man, and the second was to find out who he was working for. Finding him should be fairly easy. The second part may be harder but not impossible. He hadn't discussed the case with Allen as he normally would. Phil had been feeling like he had been letting things slide of late. Allen had said nothing. He never would, but deep down, Phil knew he wasn't the man he once was. He promised himself that if he ran into any trouble, he would call in Allen and his 'nose', but he would go it alone for now.

He had made several calls and got a few emails back, bearing slivers of the puzzle that was confronting him. Finally, he sat forward, hands flat on his desk. "I need a drink," he said to the empty room. He looked at the mess in front of him. He knew somewhere in all this was an answer. Maybe not the neat answer he would like, but an answer was there. He closed his laptop, stacked the papers in a loose order and put them in a file folder, then he stood and put the folder in the cabinet behind him. He clicked his desk lamp off, stepped from the dark room, grabbed his coat, and left.

The building had an old elevator, the slowest thing he had ever ridden in. It creaked and groaned and occasionally dropped several inches. He walked past it and took the stairs. It was only two floors, after all it would do him good. As he walked, he thought about the case. He wished he had his partner's intuition. If he had, he might have already wrapped it up. Allen was exceptional. He seemed to feel where the answer was and how to get to it, a born detective. For all the years they had worked together, Phil had always played the bumbling sidekick. He chuckled and pushed out into the night.

The night air was cool, and the forecast was for snow. There was a crispness in his nose. The first snow always made him feel like a bit of a kid and all the excitement it brought. A noise from above made him look up. It was a crow. He stared at it as it looked down on him. He couldn't remember seeing a crow in the city. And did they come out at night? He guessed they had to be somewhere. Phil watched the crow for several seconds. He became uncomfortable under the bird's gaze. With a grunt, he tore his eyes away. Dismissing the strangeness of the black shape, he walked down the street to find a bar. He did not look back.

After a couple of drinks, he went back to his quiet apartment. It was as silent as he had feared. He rubbed his eyes; the tiredness rolled over him, and within minutes of turning on the TV, he was asleep.

His dreams were nothing new. The last few months, he had spent his nights running and being chased. Allen said it was stress, but Phil had had stress dreams before. But these felt different, more urgent, and more real.

He woke in his chair with the sun just coming up and the TV still on. This was the third night in a row he had slept in that fucking chair. He felt like shit; he was still exhausted, and his back was stiff. He switched the TV off and went to shower. When he finished dressing, the coffee machine had percolated. He filled his travel mug with strong black coffee and left his apartment, locking the door behind him.

Outside, he caught a cab in front of his apartment building and was at his office in a few minutes. Allen and Phil had shared this office for over twenty years. Phil was the 'first in' this morning. This was a 'never before' event. He smiled at what Allen would likely say about that.

The small office was split into three rooms, reception was in the middle, flanked by the two offices. Phil went into his but left the door open. He wanted to see Allen's face when he walked in and saw him sitting at his desk.

Phil pulled his 'friend's' case file and ran through some details. A few of his calls and emails from yesterday had returned with some additional information, but nothing concrete. He did a few more searches based on the information he had received. He was not happy with where he was with the inquiry. He was thinking he would have to bring Allen in, after all.

He realised he was hungry. He checked his watch. It was after lunch, and neither Allen, nor Stella, the receptionist, had come in. Phil couldn't remember Allen saying anything about being out, but he was on another case, so maybe. Phil dismissed it and went for lunch.

He couldn't think of anything he wanted to eat. The Scratch in Time had great sandwiches, but at that moment, they didn't appeal. He decided he was more tired than hungry. Maybe a nap would clear things. A cab rolled by, and he hailed it. As he climbed in, he glanced up to where the crow had been the night before, remembering the strangeness he had felt.

As he sat back in the cab, he congratulated himself on his good luck with cabs today. Realisation crept over him, and he smiled. Of course, it was easy to get a cab and of course Allen hadn't come in. It was Sunday.

Back at his apartment, he took off his coat and stretched out on top of the bed with his shoes on. When he woke, his mouth was dry. He was surprised to see that night had fallen.

"Fuck." he said. How long had he slept? It was nearly 7. How could he have slept for that long? He had to admit he felt better, but he would have a hard time falling asleep tonight.

He checked his email. He had reached out yesterday to a man who worked in an insurance office and helped out with information occasionally. Phil always thought the man had far more 'shady' sources than legit. He wasn't someone he or Allen called upon too often. His price was high, but the information was always reliable. His informant had replied.

Tuesday

Phil had spent four hours waiting outside a small apartment building. The email he had received from his source told him the man he was searching for would be in this building and would leave after 7. He was confident of the information because he was sure of the source. However, it had been hours, and he was wondering if this would be the first time his informant was wrong, or had he just been too late and had missed his quarry? He had spent the money, non-refundable, of course, and he may have to pay it again. The profit on this job was shrinking. Phil cursed himself. Allen would be pissed.

He decided he would give it another half an hour and then pack it in. He needed to warm up and have a coffee. He wondered if staying another 30 minutes was even worth it. Maybe it was time to let it go. His stomach rumbled loudly, and he started thinking about food. That place over on 6th had great burgers, and maybe he'd have a beer instead of a coffee. It wasn't late after all. What...a little after 11?

Yes, that was what he was going to do. With his shoulder, he pushed off the wall and headed down the alley when the front door of the building opened. There he was the man he was searching for. He was 5' 8" or maybe 5' 10", slim, and had dark hair pushed back. He had deep-set eyes, a thin face, and he looked older than the photo Phil had, maybe 30 or even 35. Under a streetlight, the man paused to light a cigarette, turned, and walked with a purposeful stride through the cloud of smoke. It swirled around him as he went down the street, with Phil following.

The man seemed very intent on where he was going, as if he was late for an appointment. He didn't turn around and didn't look about at all. On this quiet street, it would be very easy to be spotted. To follow someone like this was difficult. Phil walked along as casually as possible. He knew he should have called in Allen, and they could have switched off.

The man hastened to the end of the street and turned right, disappearing from Phil's view. Phil hurried to the corner, then peeked around it. His quarry was already halfway down the block, walking fast, nearly running. For a minute, he thought he had been spotted, but the man never looked back, and after following him, Phil was convinced the man was late for something. He was constantly glancing at his watch. Phil kept pace, wondering what sort of meeting at this time of night would enlist this kind of behaviour. It was nearing midnight. It seemed clandestine, and probably illegal. This may be the big break Phil had been hoping for.

This could be it, the meeting that would wrap the case up. And help him fulfill the second part of the job. He got excited. He hurried forward, more determined than ever not to lose him. Ahead, the rushing man glanced down at his watch and bumped into a woman talking on her phone with a small dog at the end of a pink leash. The Dog yelped and the phone flew from her hand as she toppled to the ground. He stopped to help, then a sort of panic seemed to take him, and he bolted. The woman on the ground swore at him as she picked herself up, reaching for her phone. Phil raced past her. She swore again, but he didn't stop.

The man had slowed, then vanished. Already out of breath, Phil quickened his pace, straining to find him. He

sprinted forward and saw the back alley. At the edge, he
stopped and peered around the corner. His quarry was
walking slowly down the center, scanning the lane. With a
quick glance, Phil got a picture of the situation. There wasn't
much for cover, only one large metal garage bin halfway
between Phil and the man. Moving quietly, Phil crept along
the wall toward the bin. The man seemed very engrossed
in his search. Phil hoped the street noise behind him would
disguise his approach.

Once at the metal bin, the smell was unbelievable. Flies
buzzed around Phil as he cautiously looked around the edge.
The man was still walking slowly. Phil glanced at his watch.
It was midnight. When he looked back, the man was beside
a large, shiny black car that had driven from a cross alley.
For a minute, Phil stared. There was no cross alley. It was
impossible. Phil felt like he was dreaming. The unrealness
of the whole scene made him question what he was seeing,
made him wonder if he had somehow fallen asleep outside the
man's building and was dreaming all this.

Numbly, Phil watched the black car's back door open.
A tall, thin man unfolded from the back seat. He smiled the
predatory smile of a used car salesman ready to make a deal.
The smile broadened as they spoke, then shook hands. Beside
them, a shadow formed, taking shape like a photo, slowly
increasing in resolution one dot at a time. When fully realised,
a tall man, dressed all in black with a large-brimmed hat, stood
smiling, holding a dark book in front of him.

Phil absently waved his hand at the black flies, which
were maddening. Abruptly, the man in the suit looked straight
into his eyes. Phil flinched and ducked back behind the

garbage bin. The flies were thick. They swirled and spiralled up, more and more of them. As Phil watched, they gathered. Their hard black forms, bumping and twisting. They formed a shape then as more flies gathered, the silhouette solidified, and a man stood there smiling down at Phil. "Mr. Hammett? So nice to make your acquaintance," he said. He, too, wore a black suit and a large-brimmed hat that shaded the upper part of his face. He was smiling hugely. Phil crouched there, looking at the man who had formed out of flies! This must be a dream! Pulling his eyes away from the bizarre sight in front of him, he cautiously looked around the edge of the bin and saw all three men standing there, looking his way.

"Phil, how nice to see you," the tall man in the suit said, and waved cheerfully. "Mr. July, please invite Mr. Hammett to join us."

"Mr. Hammett, the Judge extends his invitation. Please come with me." The man made of flies grasped Phil by the arm. He was intensely strong. At the touch, Phil recoiled. He swung a massive haymaker at the man's face. It did not connect. His fist flew through the swarm of bugs, and his momentum carried him forward, falling face down on the pavement. He scrambled to his feet and ran. He had only run a couple of paces when Mr. July reappeared in front of him, all buzzing with flies and grinning like this was the greatest joke in the world. Phil pulled up short. Then without thinking, he yanked his 9 mm out, aimed center-mass, and fired point-blank. There was a loud crack. Mr. July snapped backward; his arms were thrown wide as if to embrace the bullet. His smile never left his face. When he hit the pavement, he exploded into a swarm of black flies that filled the night air. For a second, Phil looked at the spot where a body should have lain. Then he glanced back down the alley. The three men were watching him, smiling. Phil frantically raced out of the alley and down the street.

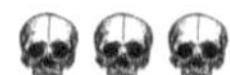

Wednesday

In a motel room, a thin strip of blazingly bright sunlight cut a white-hot line from the curtains across the carpet, the bed and the shins of the man who lay in the otherwise pitch-black room. The man was asleep on top of the covers, fully dressed, shoes on. His chest rose and fell shallowly. Slowly the crisp white line slid minute by minute, hour by hour, upward to the man's waist, then chest, finally to the man's neck where it faded, burned orange for a brief time and vanished, leaving the room and the man in complete darkness.

The phone rang. He reached for it, knowing it was bad news. "Mr. Allen Cole?" The voice on the other end was crisp and professional.

"Yes."

"My name is Constable Kowalski from Division 51. Could you come to the station to answer some questions?"

"What's this about?"

"We have an ongoing investigation. It involves your partner. Maybe you can help clear up a few things."

"It's late," Allen said for no good reason, already knowing he was going.

"Yes, it's rather urgent."

"Fine. K. Give me a half an hour."

"See you in half an hour." And the phone went dead.

With a heavy sigh, Allen sat up, swinging his legs down. He sat for a time, breathing. Then, with another sigh and a small groan, he stood. He swayed slightly and rubbed his face with both his hands. Then he turned, grabbed his puffy dark blue down-filled coat, and left the motel room.

Allen Cole was an average man of average height with an average face. If one was asked to recall him, the description would be inevitably useless. It served him well in his work. He was an investigator, a good one. He had a feel for it. Not everyone could do what he did. He knew if he followed his gut, he'd be ok. Usually, the problem could be solved with perspective. Like so many things in life, if he could change his and see things from another's perspective, he could find the solution.

Thursday

When he got to the police station, he was led down to a cell where Phil was being kept. Phil didn't look up, didn't acknowledge Allen. He hadn't responded to anyone. Allen talked to him for a while, but it was obvious something massive had happened. He was in shock and would be no help. Allen would have to find out what happened on his own.

Allen had read the report. The witness had been out walking her dog and had been run over by 'two maniacs', in quotations. She described the first man that had knocked her down as swarthy and obviously a criminal. The second man was a 'big fat man out of breath and sweating' also in quotations. She further stated she watched the men turn down an alley. After a couple of minutes, she saw the large man pull his gun out and shoot a very tall man wearing a large-brimmed hat. She had seen the muzzle flash and had watched the man fall backward. From her angle, she hadn't seen the body hit the ground. She then saw that man run down the street, away from the alley. The witness had immediately dialled 911, and later had picked Phil out of a lineup.

Phil had been found a few blocks away in a state of shock, huddled in the corner of a convenience store near the freezers. The cashier had thought he was being robbed when Phil came running in, holding his gun. Instead, he had run straight past, curled up, and was mumbling to himself. The cashier called the police. Phil's gun was taken from his hand when he was arrested, it had been fired recently, and a single round was spent.

Allen had retraced Phil's steps as best he could. He had read through the case file Phil had been working on. It all looked straightforward. Nothing would suggest the night would end the way it had. Nothing was adding up. He was following his gut, but where his gut was leading didn't make sense. And with every passing hour, it made even less sense.

The thing about 4 am in the city is it's the same in every city; not dead, but quiet. The streets are nearly empty except for cabs and garbage trucks. It's a time when the random odd people stand out, no longer lost in the crowd but revealed in the lack of cover. To find yourself walking on a city street at 4 am, some extraordinary event has either pushed you out very early or very late. Allen was out very late, and he was tired. He needed a shave and a shower to keep going. The coffee he had had earlier helped a bit. Now it sat like acid in his stomach.

He shoved his hands in his jeans as he huddled against the light snow. He refused to own a trench coat. It was such a cliche. His dark blue down-filled coat was warm, but an unfriendly bouncer at a bar two nights ago had left him with a good-sized bruise on his shoulder and a tear in his coat that disgorged small white feathers as he walked. He left a trail, like little white footprints that blended with the fresh snow briefly until the snowflakes melted and the feathers stood stark against the wet pavement.

Once again, he walked the alley. Not the second time, not even the third. This is where it had all gone horribly wrong for Phil. He knew what he was looking for. He knew it had to be somewhere here, in this alley. What he searched for was small, but it possessed great weight in the mind of the world. In order to help his friend, he needed to make sense of what had happened. It was here, in this alley. He walked with his head down, scanning. He got to the end of the street, turned, and started back again.

All at once, the night crashed down on him. He stopped walking. He looked up at the strip of dark sky framed by brick buildings. The tiny flecks of snow came falling down. His eyelashes fluttered as snowflakes landed gently on them. Like a child, he stuck out his tongue, tasting the snow. He swayed. He closed his eyes. After a minute or maybe several, he opened them and looked down. He wiped the damp from his face and rubbed his eyes.

I need to sleep; he thought.

There, where the pavement met masonry, in a corner was what he sought all these hours. A puff of feathers floated around him as he bent and picked up the small piece of brass. He brought it up into the light and examined it closely. It was a casing from a 9 mm bullet. With the casing on the end of his pencil, Allen reviewed what he knew and what he didn't. He knew Phil, his friend and partner, carried a 9 mm. Phil had been arrested, holding his gun. It had been fired recently. There was a witness that had seen him shoot a man. Phil had confessed to shooting a man point-blank, but he also told the man he shot was made of flies. Now Phil was sitting in a cell and, from the look of it, would be heading to a padded room. He wasn't making sense. Maybe he was in shock, or something far worse.

The question now, the one Allen needed to answer, was who had been shot, perhaps killed, and if killed, where was the body? Usually, dead men stay put and are easy to find, but it seemed this corpse didn't want to be found.

Allen dropped the shell casing in a small plastic bag and put it in his breast pocket. He stood, white feathers floating about him. For the first time in a long while, Allen found himself with no clear path. His gut had failed him.

He needed sleep, but he needed to find his path more. He headed back to the station to speak to Phil. Perhaps if he had been less tired, he would have noticed the man that formed in the shadows smiling wearing a large-brimmed hat.

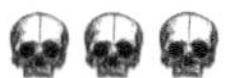

Friday

Allen returned to the police station. The cops were very accommodating, partly because of the relationship Allen had cultivated. Over the years, both Phil and Allen had helped them out, off the record, of course.

The holding cell Phil was in was one of four in a locked room. Allen went in and heard the door shut behind him with a loud chunk. He pulled a plastic chair from the wall and placed it in front of Phil's bars.

"Phil, you gotta help me. I'm at a dead end. I can't make sense of any of this."

Phil said nothing, just rocked back and forth, mumbling.

After a time, Allen put his head in his hands. He had been sitting in the hard plastic chair for a couple of hours talking, questioning, pleading with Phil, and he was getting nowhere. At one point, Phil had looked up, his eyes wide, their whites showing, and screamed about men made of flies and a black car that had driven out of the wall. Allen, taken aback, stared, mouth agape.

Finally, Allen stood and put the chair back against the wall where he had found it. He looked through the bars at his friend. He knew now Phil could not help him. He wasn't even sure Phil was in there anymore.

"I'll see you, buddy. You just hang in there. I'll find out what the hell's going on." Allen paused, looking in the cell. His friend sat on his bunk, rocking. Absently, Allen waved at a fly as he turned and pressed the buzzer on the door to be let out. He heard a sound. First, it was a buzzing mixed with a violent scuffling sound, and then a gurgling cry. Allen spun around and ran the few paces back to the cell bars.

Allen couldn't make sense of what he was seeing. Phil was struggling, his feet dangling off the ground, his hands tearing at the black hands wrapped around his neck. They held him up and were strangling him. He flailed about wildly, but to no avail. The hands were long, and the man who held Phil was very tall, very thin, dressed all in black. He wore a large-brimmed hat, and he was smiling.

As Allen watched, the man in the hat turned to look at him, and his smile widened. Never letting go of Phil, he seemed to be enjoying himself.

Behind Allen, he heard the main door being unlocked and a cop, keys rattling, came running in. Allen banged on the bars, frantic with rage. Phil's fighting slowed and became weaker until they stopped. With a final jerk, Phil hung unmoving, suspended, his legs dangled like a rag doll.

The cop was pulling at his keys, looking for the one for Phil's cell. Phil crumpled to the ground as the man in the hat disintegrated into a seething mass of flies that dropped to the floor. When the cop finally opened the cell, Phil lay dead in a pool of black flies.

Saturday

Allen sat in his office with the door open, looking across to the closed door of Phil's. With no victim and the suspect obviously mentally unstable, having committed suicide while in custody, the case had been dropped. The 'how' he had committed suicide was not mentioned. The confession was written off as the ravings of a broken mind. The witness was deemed unreliable and mistaken.

Allen was confused and angry at Phil. They had been friends for 40 years. They had gone through school, marriage, divorce, always together. It made no sense. Why hadn't he come to Allen? Why didn't he ask for help? Why had he felt like he had to solve this case on his own?

What Allen had seen in the holding cell felt like a dream. The counsellor he spoke to explained that what he saw was a coping mechanism to protect him from his close friend's suicide. He couldn't reconcile the image of the man of flies and what was written in the official report.

Phil was gone. Those words did not make sense to him. How could Phil be gone? He stepped out of the building. The realisation settled on him that he would never see Phil again, never be annoyed by his gum chewing, never share a beer or a laugh with him. He dug in his pocket for his keys to lock up. Across the street, partially hidden in the shadows, two men stood watching him. They were very tall, dressed in black. They both wore large-brimmed hats and were smiling with teeth that nearly shone skull-like in the gloom. A cab drove past as Allen turned, locked the door, and started down the steps. The two men were gone, but Allen, in the cab's headlights, had seen their faces for a flash. Of course, it was his grieving mind, but what he had seen in that flash would haunt him for the rest of his life. Those men had no eyes under their black hats.

A COLD HAND

9

ONE OF THOSE MORNINGS

Dominic had heard of people having incredibly bad days, days that were off the chart for shitty things happening. YouTube had been full of them lately. Some of the most outrageous stories of unbelievably bad things happening to people, many stacked upon one thing after another. Dominic assumed it was another 'trend' on social media. It was everywhere even on TikTok though he never went there.

Then he got fired. At first, he wasn't even sure he was fired. He had gone to work on a Tuesday morning and there had been a very close call with a semi. It had taken some time to sort things out, but he had made it to the office building only a little more than an hour late but when he went to pass his security card through the turnstile, it refused to open for him. That was the first clue this was going to be an epic bad day. In hindsight he should have started recording right then. It would have gone viral.

Then the second horrendous thing happened. Standing in the lobby with scowling security guards hovering, he had called Martha, his assistant, on his cell. She was crying when she answered. He recognised the high-pitched whimpering that passed for her weeping.

He was frustrated by the key card mix up and by her unprofessional way of answering the phone. He berated her and told her to fix this fuck up. After several minutes of silence, she came back on the phone screaming, screaming at him about what a sick bastard he was, and how could he be such a piece of shit to pull this kind scam today of all days?

Dominic stood in the lobby; mouth slack unable to understand what had just happened. Had she gone fucking mad. How could she even imagine she could talk to HIM like this and what the fuck was she going on about? He stood for several minutes staring at his phone, all the while the guards were stepping slowly forward ready to eject him.

A quick glance over his shoulder confirmed he was seconds away from being thrown out of his building, a building he had worked in for more than six years.

Thinking fast he called his boss, sure that all this would disappear the moment the head of the company was involved. The phone rang several times and a man Dominic had never heard before answered. Dominic started to explain what was happening and was very professionally cut off. The man was the boss's lawyer and advised to forget this number and never call it again. He then hung up just as two very large young men grasped him under the arms and carefully but firmly carried him from the building and with just a small, restrained push released him into the parking lot.

Dominic, confused and more than a little scared, walked to his car and sat. He sat for more than an hour trying to figure out what had just happened. He stared at his phone, looked at the other cars in the lot, watched some employees come and go, some he recognised, others he did not. He did what he knew he could, what he was sure of, and went home.

The whole drive home had an edge of the surreal. Normally he was at work on a Tuesday at ten thirty. He didn't recognise the traffic at this time of day. It was remarkably quiet and with what had just happened to him it felt like a bad 'end of the world' sci-fi movie.

He parked in his spot and got out of his car. After passing the doorman, he walked through the lobby and waited for the elevator. That's when things got worse. As was his latest habit, he was watching a new batch of horrible day videos when the doorman called to him. Dominic turned and did not recognize the man behind the counter who called him.

"Excuse me. Did you want me to announce you?" The young man said with a cautious smile.

Dominic, still confused by getting fired earlier, because that is what must have happened, looked at the man in his crisp black uniform and just said, "Huh?"

"Sir, Are you a resident?"

"I am. I am Dominic Brewer from 1204." Then anger bubbled up. "Are you asking everyone who enters the building!"

"Sorry sir. I've been instructed to. Mr. Brewer? Oh Yes, I have several messages for you."

Somewhat nervously the young doorman shuffled through his desk and with a sense of relief handed over several small pink slips of paper.

"She seemed particularly anxious to speak with you." He held up one of the slips.

Dominic looked at the name scribbled on the paper. Of course, it was his sister. She was always calling, frantic about something.

Dominic picked up the papers, smiled at the doorman and with a nod walked back to the elevator.

He flipped through the slips of paper reading the names, slightly confused by them. Why would friends and family call for him but not call his cell or work.

He stepped out of the elevator and walked silently down the carpeted hallway unsure of what was going on. He had laughed at the videos of people having a bad day. Now here he was having one himself and it wasn't funny.

He dug out his keys, slipped them in the lock and went into his apartment. Staring at the notes, he tossed the keys onto the small table at the door and went into the living room.

He groaned as he flopped down on the couch. He didn't want to talk to anyone. He didn't want to have to explain why he was home in the middle of the day, and he definitely did not want to tell anyone that he had been fired, but if he didn't call his sister back she would call again, and again. Her anxiety escalated with every minute she did not speak to him. Groaning, he dug in his back pocket and pulled out his cell. Reluctantly he found her name on the recent call list and dialled.

The phone buzzed and then went dead. He looked at it. It wasn't dead he knew. He redialled and waited. It rang twice until he heard his sister's panicked voice but then the phone made a sound he had never heard before, a sort of keening and her voice receded, getting thin with an edge of static. He strained to hear her, ultimately giving up and redialing but to no avail. He tried twice more then frustrated he dropped the phone on the coffee table and sat back unsure what to do next.

"Well, I don't have to go to work." He said to his empty apartment. "I might as well go see her."

He sat for several minutes mulling over his decision. When she was in one of her moods she was challenging to be around, but if he left her alone it would just get worse until he wasn't sure what. Something bad for sure. He stared out the window. It was grey, gloomy which matched his mood perfectly.

He had just been fired for no good reason, he reminded himself. Why wasn't he raging? Why wasn't he mad as hell? He felt mildly annoyed, nothing more.

If he thought about it, he could work himself up a bit but not enough to get on the phone and raise hell. It felt unimportant in a distant odd sort of way.

He stood and looked out across the city. So many people, just going about their lives stacked on top of one another, clawing to get ahead. Each fighting for a promotion or a raise or even recognition.

Every morning of his life he had leaped from bed ready to fight. He had succeeded by pushing others out of his way, beating a path to where he had been.

It seemed so pointless. This feeling confused him. It was foreign, almost alien. He had never had these thoughts before. They scared him, undermined who he thought he was. He had defined himself as a powerhouse, a warrior of the corporate world ready to take on the world. How could he now after this setback turn into a… what? What had he turned into?

The voice inside his head was his but he did not recognize it. It was calmer, a quieter version of himself. He searched and with a surprise, could not find the nugget of anxiety he carried with him every moment. For a brief second, he felt it again over not having it. As though it were a treasured part of him. A part of him he had nurtured, even cherished now he saw as something separate from him. An add-on that he no longer needed. With that realisation he breathed in the first clean breath he had taken since he was a small boy.

A grin spread across his face. He felt light as if he no longer had anything weighing him down. Glancing out the window he nodded to the city. He knew it to be true. He had freed himself of the burden he had clung to all these years. He could not remember why he had but he had.

His sister. Yes, he should go see her not with trepidation, but just to see her. He loved her. It would be good to talk as they had when they were young and hopeful.

Smiling, he turned away from the city and resolved to hug his sister and left his apartment.

In the hallway he saw his neighbour, Mrs. Admando and her little puff of a dog, Chérie. A pair of so thoroughly unlikeable creatures that there even had been a petition to try to oust them from the building. It did not succeed and only made the tension more tangible.

Dominic put on his customary fake smile and in a confusing moment he realised the smile was in fact real.

Mrs. Adamado's smile was in contrast, a pinched artifice of someone who, despite all evidence, was absolutely convinced she could smell shit, and was just as convinced it was coming from Dominic. Head back, nose up she stared past Dominic as though he was not in the same hallway, building or even city as she.

Dominic, unperturbed, stepped beside her and reached down to pet Chérie. The trembling white furball growled briefly then leaned into his hand, curling, its tiny tail wagging enthusiastically. Mrs. Admando looked down at him past her nose. Her brow furrowed. Chérie liked no one, especially not anyone in this building. The fact she was even allowing someone to touch her, let alone come close was unprecedented.

"Chérie seems to have taken to you… humm?" she said, unable to recall Dominic's name.

"Dominic." Dominic looked up and smiled, "How have you been Mrs. Admando?" and then without thinking he asked, "and how is your mother doing? Any better?"

A weird contortion swept across her face. She stumbled, unable to speak for a second. When she recovered, she said, "No I'm sorry to say. She has declined faster than anticipated. We are going to see her now as a matter of fact."

"When my mother passed, she no longer knew who I was nor my sister. I think that was the hardest part. Her not knowing who we were. I hate to say this, but it was almost a relief when she did go. She was no longer who I remembered." Dominic looked into the dog's eyes and knew what he had said was the truth although he had never said it out loud.

The woman seemed to shrink. No longer this battleship of a person, ploughing through the world but a woman dealing with an overwhelming amount of sadness and uncertainty.

"I…She's better," then a pause, "She's the same." Her tone changed, it lowered, became soft and warm, "Thank you for asking."

The elevator arrived and together they stepped in. A hand slipped between the closing doors and a man stepped in. He exuded a grace that Dominic had never before experienced, nor had Mrs. Adamado. She fluttered. Dominic, seeing the girl she once had surfaced for a second and then receded.

The man nodded to them and turned to face the shiny door. He was taller than Dominic, with broad shoulders and a straight back.

He watched the man, taking in the man's suit, his black hair stacked high. The way he held himself straight but not as though he was uncomfortable, more like he was too comfortable, too sure of his place; as if he owned the world.

The elevator shuttered and started its slow descent. Dominic glanced sideways at Mrs. Admando. She stood pressed tight against the dark mirrored wall trying to disappear. She felt the presence of this man just as he did.

Dominic looked back; his breath caught. The man had turned and was looking straight at him.

After several awkward moments, the man's face split into an easy smile.

"Dominic. So nice to see you."

Dominic stared open-mouthed. "I… I… Who are you?"

The man's smile broadened. His teeth were very white. "I have many names, but you may call me…"

Just then Mrs Adamado screamed. Dominic's head twisted to look at her. Her mouth worked but no sound came out. The whites circled her irises bright and shiny. One hand came up to cover her mouth, the other pointed at the floor by Dominic's feet. Dominic followed the shaking finger and looked down. The man in the suit chuckled when Dominic saw his legs ended just below his pant legs as if his legs had been cut off. Experimentally he lifted his left leg. Beside him, Mrs Adamado was making odd keening noises.

His leg came out of the floor fully intact as though the floor was not there. Carefully he put his foot down on the surface and stepped up on the floor of the elevator.

He stood staring down at the floor. He looked at Mrs. Adamado who had gone silent. The man in the suit smiled at Dominic.

"It's going to get worse." He indicated the solid floor Dominic stood on. "As you start to forget."

"Forget? What are you talking about?"

The elevator shuddered to a stop. Mrs. Adamado bolted for the door, squeezing through before the doors had fully opened. The two men watched. The man in the suit turned back to Dominic, eyebrows raised, smiling. "She seemed upset."

"What do you mean, forget? Forget what?"

The man in the suit watched Dominic for a moment then his smile shifted, saddened. He turned and stepped from the elevator. Dominic followed, stepping carefully across the threshold to the tiled lobby.

On the street, the man stopped to watch people walking by.

"People spend their lives reminding themselves who they are, where they are. They make an agreement with themselves, with everyone they know, with the world. The 'real world' is that agreement." He turned to Dominic, "but now you are beginning to forget your agreement, the lie that was your life."

Dominic stared, puzzlement creasing his forehead.

Somehow, he was sitting in his car driving down a darkened street. Ahead was a brightly lit club. Massive letters on the marque said, "the Acheron Lounge".

"That's where you need to be." The man sat beside him. He nodded toward the club. Dominic turned to look at the man, surprised to see him sitting beside him in his car but they weren't in his car. They were standing on the street in front of the club.

Dominic looked at the glass doors, at the lights overhead that seemed too bright to look at. Behind him a cab slid by.

Then he was standing inside the club and the man in the suit was talking.

"I will leave you here. Jean will take care of you."

Slowly as though underwater Dominic turned to the man standing on his other side. He too was smiling.

"Who was that man?" He asked when he realised the man in the suit was no longer with them.

"That was Mr. White. Don't worry. It's not business as usual but we'll get you sorted out." He said putting his hand on Dominic's shoulder.

"I don't understand. What's going on? Am I dreaming?"

"Dreaming? No Dominic this is not a dream. Come I'll take you to the river."

"Ok". Dominic said feeling removed.

Then he was alone. He knew he was more alone than he had ever been. He stood on a dark shore of a black river, cool black sand beneath his feet and a star scattered overhead. In the dark along the river were other people. All single like him, all alone. He stared around watching the pale individuals looking as lost as he felt.

A line from a song he loved long ago came to him
"I'm wet and dead but at least I'm not old."

NO
HUNTING

10

And now some other stuff

BACK HOME DIRECTIONS

Well, s'pose I kin getcha pointed in da right direction. Let me see nows. Ya the quickest way would be ya cut through Dutch Helgason north quarter an cross the crik but you can't do that right now on accounting' da waters too high course if it were late summer wouldn't be no trouble.

Iffin you head down the road here a piece, just past the old grainery that Sylias built, turn right and go maybe 'nother 5 mile or so. Come to da Cherry ridge crossin' where the old school usta be, den ya turn left agin. No wait that'll get you to the Peterson's farm an you don wanna be messin' with ol' John Peterson. You go hisself a mean disposition and a 12 gange.

Naw you wanna make ah right back at the ol' school yard, Yessir that'll do 'er. Now if you see Stanley ol pickup truck in da ditch you've gone to far Wacha wanna do is turn left at the corner before. You'll see it. It's the turn with the 'NO HUNTIN' sign although it's kinda hard ta read with all the bullet holes in it. Anyways uz gotta turn there an go 'nother mile or so.

Wait, where's it you tryin' ta git to, agin?

In late 2005, I had spent some time writing a series of songs. At the time I was surrounded by talented musicians and was inspired. I approached my friend Frank Prather with the idea to write and produce an album together. Frank is a brilliant singer/songwriter, with the gritty voice I thought would lend well to what I had envisioned for the lyrics. He added music and sang them several times on stage. We are still working toward an album however like so many worthy projects life gets in the way.

Here are a few of the songs.

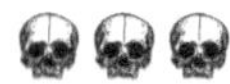

New Truck

He rolls out of bed and stumbles as he gets up
His dick is hard and everything smells like beer
Scratches his balls with calloused hands
Finds the cleanest cup in a sink of week old dishes
His bootlaces drag he runs his fingers through greasy
hair
Puts on a greasy baseball cap Slams the door as he leave
He lights up a smoke as he starts his truck
It rumbles and rattles down the gravel road
With barely readable letters on the door
No colour mud grey and black
Well the sun rises in a cloud of dust that follows him
There's an old blanket over a torn seat
He coughs and spits and snorts spends the whole day
swearing and grunting
Tonight he'll get drunk and if he's lucky
He'll get laid if he's got the money
Expectations are few but he keeps dreaming
Someday he'll get a new truck someday he'll get a new
truck
The day ends at the strip club

One more faceless man in the crowd
20 bucks gets him a woman up close, soft pale almost touchable
Her sent cuts through his oily smell
His rough hands inches away from soft white flesh
His drunk hungry stares
Looks like money to hardened eyes and practised smiles
60 bucks later and a brief slip into fantasy
Another beer and a longing look he heads to the door
Tonight he got drunk but not so lucky
He leaves feeling hungry and empty
Expectations are few but he keeps dreaming
Someday he'll get a new truck Someday he'll get a new truck
He staggers through the door his pockets are empty
His dog growls at him and he growls back
They're more like best friends than either of them would admit
His head's gonna hurt tomorrow
Against his face he feels the coolness of the toilet seat
He throws up gets up stumbles and falls into his spinning bed
With visions of crisp vinyl sparkling chromes spinning mags
Smelling that new vehicle smell
Tomorrow he'll get drunk and if he's lucky

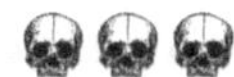

Waitress at the Smeaton hotel

pulling back his cap, his face black with dust sweat cuts
lines down his face, his short wet hair sticks to his forehead
he squints back at the field, another hour and over to the
south quarter
his belly hangs over his big square buckle and from the
seat of his tractor he sees his life move past him
but he dreams of
the waitress at the Smeaton hotel tight jeans and a loose
white shirt when she leans over to wipe the table he can smell
her down her shirt a flash of a nipple he'd stay all day

but the fields need tending, machinery needs fixing,
there's an auction at the old Peters farm, not many
friends still farming,
it feels wrong to bid on machinery that used to belong to
a friend
but the bank is selling it off, and he could use a new
seeder,afterwards he goes for a coffee

The waitress at the Smeaton hotel tight jeans and a loose
white shirt when she leans over to wipe the table
he can smell her down her shirt a flash of a nipple
he'd stay all day
but he should get home, his wife screams at him,
if there's beer on his breath
never enough money, never enough of anything
she comes to bed all creams, curlers

the waitress at the Smeaton hotel smiles at him with a
knowing look when she leans over to kiss him he can smell
her
her young body soft against his he'll stay all night

I ran into him the other day.
He said he was driving truck out of Saskatoon and

Was doing some wielding here and there.
He didn't mention his marriage had ended.
He didn't mention the waitress.
I knew she had moved out east.

HERO

He sat beside his father cold vinyl bench seat of the
pickup still a boy, between his uncle and his dad
hot dusty miles passed
gravel pinging off the bottom of the truck
the radio crackled, his uncle passed the beers and they
laughed, oh how they laughed
Chorus:
his dad was his hero racing down the gravel roads
large tanned arms smelling of varsal, cigarette hanging
out of his mouth
left arm handing out the window and a beer between his
legs
his dad was his hero
they told stories, yes they told stories women and drunk
nights, fast cars and fights each story a little better than the
last each beer making them grow
he felt so much a part of it
he felt so grown up
just like his dad
Chorus:
But when at home mom yelled
he always felt bad
but he was mostly asleep cold and wanting bed
his dad carried him to bed, talking softly smiling but
never remembering what was said and he would sleep a man
in a boys body

Aunt Sadie

> Sitting in her room with her keepsakes
A knitted blanket over her knees
All the chatter fades
Long ago she learned
People leave you alone when you're asleep
She still has on a sweater
She catches herself in the mirror
Her bluish hair all flat on one side
She curses softly as she pushes her walker to the
bathroom
It's almost time for bingo
At least she's got a chance for some change
And she remembers Jack
And she remembers Jack
Aunt Sadie was bom in 1914 the year the Titanic sunk
Her parents came over two years before
Free land in the north to farm
A chance to get out of the poverty
But Sadie didn't know about that
She grew up with dirt walls and dirt floor
Working from sunup to sun down
These things she remembers sitting in her chair
Pretending to sleep
And she remembers Jack
With dark curly hair
And his thin moustache
The roar of his 36 Ford
With the windows all the way down
She sits beside him
The stick shift between her knees
Her tight sweater over pointed bra
Just the way he liked her
Oh how fast he drove
And she remembers Jack
Ya she remembers Jack

His big hands all over her
She remembers the fire
The smell of homemade whiskey on his breathe
The look of want on his face
She loved those busy hands

She remembers Jack
She remembers Jack
Big flashy smile
His smooth promises
His roving eye
On the blonde that night
Jack would say it's nothing
Don't ya be so stupid?
Even as her belly grew
Pretty soon Jack stopped coming around
But Tom was there to make an honest woman of her
Yes Tom was a fine husband all those years
Fists and all
But Sadie remembers Jack
Sadie remember Jack
She loved those busy hands
She remembers the fire
She remembers Jack
She remembers Jack

R A JACOBSON

THIS IS WHERE HE GREW UP

a roadside stop at the edge of town
it was his dad's restaurant
it was his first job
it was never to be his last
once he had the dream
a girl and all was in the bright future
from behind the counter,
like some great story he had once
then the girl left she took with her the dream
but that wasn't his end and it wasn't closing time
but it sure felt close and he watched
the comings and goings of each of his childhood friends
util none were around
minutes marked by the wiping of yellowed counter
dog eared menu never changing once this place was
known for its food
 in way he guesses it still is
there are the regulars some knew his dad
the ones who haven't taken that
long slow ride in the black shinny Cad
some just started coming and never stopped
he served them coffee and pie maybe eggs over easily
And tells his tale anyone who's got the time anyone
but his life is here
in the stories that are told
the lies stretched for his benefit
he sees what his life is not
when no one is here
he dreams the dream
Remembers The girl
Not closing time yet
losing time and remembers

A COLD HAND

Thank you for all the love and support.
This would never have been possible without you.
Sunniva Foley
Noah Zacharin
Justin Ramsden
Jeff Bessner
Mike Jacobson
Maite Jacobson
Mercedes Jacobson
Laura Fernandez
Laura Byrne
Matt Byrne
Julian Kent
Am
Ken Cade
Peter Boyd
Satchel Boyd
Scott Petri
Pat Hodgson

About the Author

After leaving the north forests and farmland of Saskatchewan, Rick headed to Calgary and the Alberta College of Art. After 4 years of hard work, he came out confused and somewhat lost. Now what? Rick has been a bouncer (1 week), he has been a radio switcher (1 night) he worked at the CBC (1 month) he was a stuntman (2 action movies that he never saw but he's not alone in that) he modelled briefly (he was the Jolly Green Giant for a time). Rick has built houses, packed groceries, cut grass, he has written children's books (4) illustrated children's books (19). He has worked as an illustrator, a writer, a designer and a painter.

Rick has won awards for his work in advertising and publishing including the Ruth Schwartz Award, the Amelia Frances Howard-Gibbon Award and numerous national and international awards including the Toronto Art Directors' Awards, Communication Arts Magazine's Award of Excellence, American Illustration Award of Excellence, and the New York Art Directors' Award of Excellence. He has been featured in Smithsonian magazine and in The Artist's Magazine. His commissioned portraits include Margaret Atwood, Robertson Davies, Christopher Ondaatje, and David Thomson.

Rick has two collections of short stories from a HARD PLACE, 'A Single Round' and 'A Lead Pill'.

For HARD PLACE updates, sign up at deadcatstud.io.

In the dark where two dusty back roads cross a black car sits waiting. The man inside will make a deal he has many times before and will again. He is known in these parts as The Judge.
Folk go to him when they have a powerful need, a want that can't be satisfied any other way. Some are too young to know better, others are desperate and still others just plain stupid. His price is high and many never believe they will have to pay it, but the bill comes due eventually. There is no escape. No lead pill that can free you. Once struck the deal is all that remains.

Stories from a HARD PLACE is an anthology podcast.

A SINGLE ROUND is a collection of stories from Hard Place. Fully illustrated.
Stories of moonshine and shotguns, obsession and transcendence, love and darkness, and the blindness of human desire. Each tale follows a painful path to one ultimate realization: the devil's deal always ends badly, often with a single round.

My Gran used to say, "There are times when the only way out is a lead pill." These are stories when things got that bad.
A LEAD PILL is the second collection of short stories from a HARD PLACE.
Stories of loneliness and betrayal, of false hope and shattered dreams, of gifts and regrets, of love and accidental kindness.
Each story follows separate paths that lead to the understanding that sometimes the only solution is a lead pill.

"knocked the wind out of me"

"A thrilling and violent tale about how the Devil always wins."

"A nail-biting hard place to be."

"It was gripping right from the start."

"raw and candid"

"It kept me at the edge of my seat."

"Kept me up all night!"

"It's a must read!"

A cursed man tricks the Devil with Death's help.

Demons and deals, motorbikes and taverns, crossroads and consequences. Moonshine and shotguns and two men in love with the same woman 30 years apart.

When your day starts with a close friend stopping by and trying to kill you, you know the rest of your week could only get better. Unfortunately, for Jacob, that's not the case.

When Mr. White and The Judge meet at the crossroads, Jacob and Matt could lose everything.

We have a new site just for the Hard Place series, scan this QR code to get immersed in the Hard Place series. You can find all the books in the series and swag. Yes, we have swag!

If you have read Hard Place and would like to leave a review please scan this QR code.

www.ingramcontent.com/pod-product-compliance
Lightning Source LLC
Chambersburg PA
CBHW032121050726
47591CB00011B/1363